"I'm not sha[ring] with you,"

Sarah protested inside the hotel room.

Scott locked the door behind them. "I didn't think you would object."

"We met only yesterday."

"We met twenty years ago," he reminded her softly, his eyes revealing all his longing for her, "and we slept together then."

"Oh, well, if you sleep with your clothes on like you did then . . ."

"I registered us as Mr. and Mrs. MacInnes," Scott murmured. "I saw how the men in the saloon looked at you. I don't want any misunderstandings about who you belong to."

To Sarah, it sounded right for Scott to say she belonged to him. In the twentieth century it would sound chauvinistic, but it was different here.

Scott reached for her. "I've waited for you most of my life, Sarah. Come to me."

Dear Reader,

Who among us hasn't dreamed of living in a different age?

Certainly Regan Forest, one of our most innovative writers, did from the moment she walked into the Bird Cage Theater in Tombstone, Arizona. She says she could sense its ghosts and was compelled to write *Borrowed Time*—especially since the *New York Times* called the Bird Cage in its heyday "the wildest, wickedest night spot between Basin Street and the Barbary Coast."

We are pleased to make this moving love story an Editor's Choice—the mark of a bold, sexy Temptation tale with a twist. Coming in February and March 1993, we have two Editor's Choice stories by bestselling author JoAnn Ross—"taking you to the final frontier, where no one has been before!"

We hope you enjoy *Borrowed Time* and all of our wonderful Temptation books.

Yours sincerely,

Birgit Davis-Todd
Senior Editor

P.S. We love to hear from our readers!

BORROWED TIME

REGAN FOREST

Harlequin Books

TORONTO • NEW YORK • LONDON
AMSTERDAM • PARIS • SYDNEY • HAMBURG
STOCKHOLM • ATHENS • TOKYO • MILAN
MADRID • WARSAW • BUDAPEST • AUCKLAND

For Heidi, with love

Author's Note: Many thanks to the owner of the Bird Cage Theater, William M. Hunley, Jr., for his enthusiastic support of this project, and for introducing me to some of the Bird Cage Theater's ghosts.

Published November 1992

ISBN 0-373-25518-7

BORROWED TIME

Prologue

ALL HER LIFE she'd believed it a dream. Now, standing in the musty Bird Cage Theater in Tombstone, Arizona, Sarah Christianson knew the strange memories were true, knew she'd been here before.

A hundred years had not silenced the ghosts. She could still hear the insincere laughter of the "ladies of the night" who'd plied their trade in the small, curtained "cages" suspended from the ceiling. She could still hear the music of the grand piano at the foot of the stage where dancing girls had once frolicked. Gunshots still echoed from the streets outside.

Shivering in the dim light, Sarah made her way past the museum relics—nineteenth-century artifacts and old photographs—and walked up the stairs onto the stage. The narrow steps leading to the catwalks behind the balcony cages were exactly as she remembered. The old stage props were gone, the curtains in rags. She stood amid the few tourists, trying to understand what it all meant. If she had really spent two time-lost days here, then that boy—the boy she'd loved—was real and not a dream. He would have grown into a man and died of old age long ago. And maybe all his life he'd wondered why she had disappeared so suddenly and so completely.

Her eyes brimming with tears, Sarah made her way outdoors and onto Allen Street. In her dream she'd been told that the people who walked there were so wicked that the street was forbidden yet she'd walked there with him—with the only man she'd ever really loved. A man? A mischievous and very mysterious boy who'd loved her. . . .

A boy who'd lived here in Tombstone long ago.

1

LOOKING BACK over her childhood, Sarah had asked herself a thousand times if her grandmother had known about the incredible secret hidden in her attic. If she had, why would she have let a child go up there? Or had she somehow understood that it was Sarah's destiny to climb the stairs that had led her into the past?

Now it was too late to ask. She would never know.

SARAH REMEMBERED that attic very well; it was a mysterious place abrim with treasures. She'd not been allowed anywhere near it when she was small, but today, on her eleventh birthday, she had permission to climb the high stairway to the murky, low-ceilinged room.

The single naked bulb had burned out, so the only light came in through the high, round windows under the gables. Dust particles danced in the pale rays. Ghosts might lurk in a loft like this, Sarah thought, glancing at the shadows in every corner. Her attention was caught by an old wicker baby pram, a white wooden high chair with pink and blue trim, and a collection of crates and trunks.

Tingling with excitement at the thought of the unknown, Sarah opened the lid of one old trunk and removed the tissue paper that lay on top, protecting silk scarves and a dress of linen lace. A bride's dress. She lifted it out and held it in front of her, wondering who had worn the dress and when.

Underneath it, carefully placed among the folds of cotton petticoats, lay a small object wrapped in lavender tissue paper. Curious, Sarah unwrapped it, to find a delicate china bird. White with pink and yellow brush strokes over its wings, the little bird warmed her palm as she lifted it from its paper nest.

"How pretty!" she exclaimed.

The light from the high windows caught its sheen, the way Christmas lights illuminate the ornaments on a tree. The bird reminded her of a tree ornament, but it had no hook for hanging. She turned it over and over in her hand, imagining the bird she could hear warbling in the topmost branches outside the window was this bird singing.

Sarah caressed the little bird, running one finger over its wings, along its graceful neck to the beak and felt a sudden prick; a tiny drop of blood on her finger. Her head reeled with a sudden dizziness, and all she could see was the sparkling dust in the beam of light. She felt herself growing faint and falling into blackness.

MOMENTS LATER the blackness lifted; it was as though rays of light were rising from the bird in her hand, filling the room with sun again.

But this wasn't her grandmother's house. Sarah looked about in alarm. A heavy curtain formed a wall in front of her, and from somewhere beyond came the sounds of voices and laughter. On the left was a railed stairway leading downward. There was furniture—a narrow cot, a dresser and some chairs and tables—but it was pushed to the back of the room, as if it were only stored there.

Where on earth was she? How did she get here? A chill of fright surged through her at the sound of footsteps on the stairway. A blond woman appeared and stopped abruptly. "How did you get in here?" she asked. Sarah saw that the woman was not much older than a high school girl, but hardly dressed like one. She wore her hair upswept and curled. Her dress was of maroon satin, cut low in front, and edged with a wide collar of off-white lace. Her stockings were black, above high-heeled boots, like those women often wore in Western movies. She took a step toward Sarah. "And what are you doing with my bird? How dare you get into my things and steal?"

Sarah looked down at the glass bird in her hand. "I—I didn't steal it. . . ."

"Give it back!" The young woman's face contorted with anger. "I put my belongings back here on the stage to keep them safe, not to have some brat—" She grabbed the bird from Sarah's hand.

Sarah's mind whirled; fear warred with confusion. It was such a realistic dream, but how could she have fallen so suddenly and soundly asleep?

Looking down at the figurine, the young woman was muttering something. "Oh. This bird isn't mine. This one has pink and yellow on the wings." She looked up, clearly mystified. "My Lord...the matching bird! How can this be?"

Sarah stared at her.

"Where did you get it?" The anger was gone from the young woman's voice, and only awe remained.

"From my grandmother," Sarah answered.

"Where is your grandmother? Where do you come from?"

"From California."

"California? You've just arrived in Tombstone, then?"

"I don't know. I don't know how I got here.... I don't even know where I am. Where is Tombstone?"

The woman's voice softened. "You're a runaway! But to find your way here, to the Bird Cage, I mean, there must be something magical happening." She walked to a far corner of the room, her boot heels clicking on the wooden floor. Music and male voices still echoed from somewhere outside.

"My name is Josie," the woman said, kneeling to open an old leather suitcase in the corner. "What's yours?"

"Sally," Sarah replied. It was her family's nickname for her.

"Sally. I'm sorry I accused you of stealing. I stashed some of my things here because someone is robbing the houses on my street." From the suitcase she pulled another glass bird. "Here," she said, pointing with a long, red fingernail. "If you notice the wings, the brushed color is blue and green, while on yours it's pink and yellow. These birds are a pair, no doubt about it."

"I don't understand," Sarah said.

"Neither do I. This bird was given to me in Dodge City by an old Gypsy who said it had special powers. He said if I ever found the other one, I would have found my true and forever love. Well, isn't that a crock? What I find is a lost kid!" She smiled. "I never believed in miracles, anyhow. Do you?"

"Yes."

Josie laughed. "You're young yet. Life hasn't kicked you hard enough." She rose, still holding her bird. "Why are you wearing boys' clothes and those odd shoes?"

Sarah looked at her sandals. Since when were jeans and a T-shirt considered boys' clothes?

"Do you have any other clothes with you?"

"No."

Josie put her arm gently around Sarah's shoulders. "Look, pet, I understand. I was a runaway myself, not much older than you. In actual fact I still am a runaway. I ran from a mean husband in Dodge City. I'll help you and not give you away. But you can't stay here in the Bird Cage. I'm going to talk to someone who can offer you a place to sleep and some food. And something respectable to wear. Good Lord, if you didn't have those pretty blond curls, people might think you're a boy."

Sally trembled on the verge of tears. The dream was rapidly turning into a nightmare, one she wanted to end—quickly.

Seeing her frustration, Josie patted her shoulder. "It'll be all right, pet. You just stay right here. Don't go up front. If people come, just say you're waiting for Josie. I won't be long. Here, take my bird. It's yours to keep…my way of apologizing for misjudging you. The pair should be together, anyway, the Gypsy told me. By some weird coincidence, you found the mate to yours. So keep them together. Maybe they'll bring *you* true and forever love."

Sally heard such deep sadness in the young woman's voice that her heart filled with pity. Accepting the bird, she watched Josie disappear down the railed back stairway then studied the two china birds. Except for the slight difference in coloring, they were identical. She held them to the light, admiring their sheen, their delicate beauty. "A pair," she whispered, holding them together so that their wings touched.

Suddenly she heard a rustling from just outside the thick, red curtain in front of her. A face peered cautiously through—the face of a boy about her age. He stared at her, gazed about the room, then spoke in a half whisper.

"Hey. Are you the only one back here?"

"Yes."

"How come?" He slid hurriedly through the curtain, as if afraid of being seen. He wore faded jeans and cowboy boots and a dirty shirt. His eyes were as blue as the summer sky, and his dark brown hair was un-combed. His was the most handsome face Sally had ever seen. He looked at her with curiosity, curiosity and something more. His blue eyes were friendly, accepting. "What are you doing here?"

Because she had no idea how to answer, she asked the question back. "What are *you* doing here?"

He smiled. "Snooping. I wanted to see what the stage was like. I sneaked in through the saloon and nobody said anything, but then I saw a couple women looking at me like they were ready to kick me out, so I came back here to see if there was a place to hide behind the stage." He grinned. "I thought I might even see some dancing girls, but I guess it's too early for a show."

Stage? Dancing girls? Sarah crossed the room, parted the curtain behind him, peeked out and gasped. Just below was an enormous room filled with tables and chairs, like a restaurant. At the far end was a saloon full of men crowded around a long bar. The sides of the room were lined with balcony cages, elaborately decorated with bright blue and gold wallpaper and framed by red velvet curtains.

"You shouldn't be in here," he said.

"Why not? What is this place?"

"It's the Bird Cage Theater. Everyone knows that."

"The what?" Josie had kept saying something about a bird cage but Sarah hadn't understood. She'd thought it had something to do with the little china birds.

The boy looked at her strangely. After a moment he turned, walked to the backstairs rail and looked down.

"What's down there?" she asked.

"A room where guys play poker. It looks almost the same!"

"The same as what?"

He turned and shrugged. "The same as I thought it would. There's a game going on down there, but I think I can get out the back door this way. I gotta go."

She watched him move around the railing. He hurried down the steps and disappeared.

A cold silence enveloped the empty, curtained-off stage. The boy had left so quickly; he was uneasy about being here. Feeling a similar unease, even more than before, Sarah sat down on the cot, which she knew now was a prop, like the other pieces of furniture that were standing around. The boy in cowboy boots seemed to have popped up here just because he wanted to see the place that was off-limits to kids. What was so awful about it? Why had he and Josie both said she shouldn't be here? Because of the cowboys out there drinking? *How had she managed to fall so soundly asleep that she could know she was dreaming and not wake up?*

She sat with only the birds for company for long, dragging minutes, until she again heard rushing footsteps on the back stair. It wasn't Josie, but the boy, whose head appeared through the bars of the railing.

"How come you're still here?" he asked her.

"I don't have any place to go."

"That's what I figured. You acted lost." His understanding smile was a gift.

"I am," she admitted.

"Look," he said gently. "Kids aren't allowed in here. It's a bad place. Really bad women work here."

Sarah's heart lurched. Josie worked here, she thought, and Josie was nice. "What do you mean, bad?"

He scowled. "You know—ladies of the night."

"I *don't* know!" Sarah protested, but had seen enough movies to have some idea, at least.

The boy was plainly in a hurry. "Come on. Let's get out of here!"

"Why did you come back?"

"For you. 'Cuz you're lost. Before long some show people might come in to use the stage. You don't want to be caught in here, take my word."

"But where are you going?"

"To see if Wyatt Earp is in town. Hurry up!"

She had heard the name before. He was a gunfighter. She looked at the birds. "I can't carry these, they might break."

She hid them carefully, side by side, between some two-by-four studs in a far corner of the stage, where she hoped no one would find them before she came back to meet Josie, as she'd promised.

"I'll go for a little while," Sally said, "but then I have to come back. I told Josie I would wait."

He nodded impatiently and led the way down the steps. Sarah noticed the word Lucky carved in dark letters on the back of his leather belt. "Is that your name? Lucky?"

"Yeah. What's yours?"

"Sally."

In the smoky room at the bottom of the stairs seven men sat around a poker table. Most wore large mustaches and had somber faces; the very sight of them frightened Sarah. On the table were whiskey glasses and full ashtrays. Butts of cigarettes and cigars were all over the floor, and the area smelled of cigar smoke, spilled whiskey and sweat. The men were not talking much; only one or two glanced at the youngsters, but said nothing.

Lucky hurried, almost running, between the low railing and the closed doors on the opposite wall to reach the exit as quickly as possible; Sally was right behind him.

Outside was a long, narrow, wood frame structure. "It's an outhouse," Lucky said. "Twenty-one seats. I counted them." He pointed to the building just behind the outhouse. "And that's a jail."

They stepped onto a street that had covered sidewalks and wooden buildings on both sides. To Sarah it looked almost unreal. Yet the street was teeming with the sounds and smells of real life—horses kicking up dust, and riders wearing wide-brimmed hats, kerchiefs at their necks. She heard laughter from the Bird Cage and from other saloons across the street. The sun was bright in the morning sky. The roofs over the wooden sidewalks cast dark shadows over the storefronts. Sarah was too surprised to speak. An old-fashioned cowboy town! Josie had called it Tombstone.

Lucky didn't seem to know the town very well. He seemed to be interested in each storefront they walked by—a cigar store, a jewelry store, a restaurant, another saloon...

Sarah could feel people staring at them. There were no women and no other children walking on this street, only men with mustaches and beards, many of them wearing guns.

A tall man wearing his pant legs tucked into the top of his boots approached them and stopped. "You kids got some business on Allen Street?"

"Maybe," Lucky answered defiantly.

"I think not," the tall man said. "This ain't no territory for kids." He was studying Sarah, she knew. "Especially little girls. You know better."

Lucky grabbed her hand and hurried past the stranger without another word. "I forgot that," he whispered. "Girls don't walk on this street...except the bad ones."

That again. She hated the way he said it. "How do you know only bad women walk here?"

"My mom told me. She told me a lot of things about Tombstone."

"Tombstone, Arizona? Is that where we really are?" Josie had told her, but having Lucky confirm the fact made the idea sink in. How could she be in Tombstone, Arizona?

He took her hand again and stepped into the street. "Yeah! Where did you think?"

"You don't live here?"

"No. I live on a ranch over west some miles." Lucky broke into a trot and she followed, her feet kicking up dust. They ran to the opposite side of the street, past the Oriental Saloon and around the corner into a side street. Here the buildings were smaller. They passed a bank, three grocery stores and another theater.

"Are you looking for something?" she asked.

"A gun shop."

"Why?"

"Because I've already been here a day and night without a gun, and I just figured out how I can get one." He looked at the sign at the end of the block. "Fremont Street. Yeah, I know where we are. Come on, this way."

He paused at the window of a millinery store. "Look at these stupid hats, Sally! I bet you'd never wear a hat like that."

She giggled, trying to picture herself grown-up and trying on these monstrosities of feathers and bows. "Never in a million years!"

Just past the milliner's Lucky found a gun shop. She followed him inside. The proprietor, standing behind the counter reading a newspaper, looked at them over the top of his small, round glasses.

Sally stretched over the counter, on tiptoe, to read the date on the newspaper, the *Tombstone Epitaph*— February 2, 1882. Almost a hundred years ago! She felt numb. She really was in Tombstone, Arizona in 1882.

"Help you, son?"

"I'm looking for a Colt 44, single action. Used, if you got any."

"I've got some."

"Let's see one with a seven-and-a-half-inch barrel."

"Yeah, sure." The proprietor opened a case, and Sally saw Lucky's attention zoom in on a revolver with a polished black handle.

"Ain't that barrel a mite long for your size, son?"

"I've shot long barrels before," the boy answered, turning the gun over in his hand, not looking at the man.

"It was owned by an outlaw name of Cuss Bradley, who shot up the Crystal Palace ceiling and was run out of town. That's all I can tell you about this particular revolver. I've got others—"

"I like this one," Lucky said. He laid down the gun, unfastened his belt, and snapped off his shining Western buckle. "The buckle is solid silver," he said. "It's worth two guns, but I'll trade it for this revolver, a holster and shells and a little loose cash."

The proprietor gawked at the buckle. It was engraved with designs around the edge of a raised steer head. "I ain't never seen nothing like it," he said.

"It's worth plenty," the boy answered. "But it's all I got with me. I got no money. Just this."

"You got a deal then."

"I need two boxes of shells and six dollars cash, too."

"Six dollars? Can't do it."

"Then I'll find somebody else to trade with. I need money for food."

The man eyed the silver buckle again, pursed his lips and nodded.

Lucky was strapping on the gun belt in minutes. He asked, "Are the Earps in town? Is Wyatt?"

The tradesman adjusted his eyeglasses and grinned. "You ain't planning to take on the Earp brothers, let's hope."

"That's not even funny," Lucky answered. "I want to see them in person. I heard all the stories."

"You and everybody else." The shop owner polished the buckle against his arm. "Wyatt and James and Virgil been living at the Cosmopolitan Hotel since the bad trouble started, after the gunfight when the McLaurys and Billy Clanton was killed. Virgil was ambushed outside the Oriental Saloon a few weeks ago. Shattered his left arm bad. Doc Goodfellow says he won't never fight again."

"Everyone has heard about the ambush," Lucky said. He slid the long-barreled revolver into its holster, and took Sarah's hand to lead her outside. She was counting. It was the third time he had taken her by the hand, and each time it sent a little thrill through her.

Once outside, she stopped. "What do you need a *gun* for?"

"It's a real mean town, you know, Sally. A guy has to be armed. Men get shot on the street all the time— like you just heard."

"But you're just a kid!"

"I'm eleven. Eleven is about grown."

Since when? she thought. But then, what did she know about the olden days?

They were in the *olden days*, and it didn't feel one bit like a dream. "This is crazy. This is crazy," she repeated, as they continued along the street.

He pointed straight ahead. "At the end of the next block is where the Earp brothers and Doc Holliday shot the McLaury brothers and Billy Clanton. You know about that gunfight."

"No," she answered.

"You're kidding! Next you're going to tell me you never rode a horse."

"Never."

"Cripes! Where are you from?"

"Los Angeles."

"Oh." He stopped suddenly. "We passed a livery stable back there. Let's get a horse."

"For six dollars?"

He shook his head. "We probably couldn't buy a horse for a hundred dollars. I meant we'll borrow one."

He swung around and climbed a fence into an enclosure where four horses were corraled. Lucky looked them over carefully and decided he wanted the sorrel mare.

"Aren't you going to *ask?*" Sally rasped, crouching beside the gate.

"They'd say no if I asked. I'll just leave a note in the tack shed, saying we'll bring back the mare in a half hour. I don't see anybody around."

Moments later he emerged from the shed with a bridle and saddle. "We'd better not ride bareback if you never did this before. You might fall off." He saddled the mare, unlatched the gate, then climbed back over to fasten the latch again from the inside.

Sarah allowed herself to be helped up and onto the blanket behind the saddle. She clung to Lucky's waist and thrilled to the feel of the horse under them, the smell and the squeaking of the leather saddle. He was a real cowboy, like those in the movies! And even more handsome! Careful not to touch the gun, she held on to him, feeling the muscles of his torso react instinctively to the movements of the horse.

Sarah knew she was in love.

They rode along the outlying streets of the town. It had frightened her when he said they would be in big trouble if the owner of the horse happened to see them. She began to worry about leaving the Bird Cage Theater after she'd told Josie she would wait.

"If you're worried about it, I'll take you back there," her cowboy offered. They rode down Sixth Street, along rows of small shacks Lucky said he had heard called the "red-light district." There were no red lights that they could see. He stopped the horse near the twenty-one-seat outhouse behind the Bird Cage.

Once dismounted, he helped her down.

"Do we have to go past the cardplayers again?"

"Yeah," he answered, tying up the horse with practiced ease. "But none of them said anything to us before, so just stay close to me."

Inside a serious game was in progress. One player scowled when he looked up. Lucky met his gaze bravely and hurried toward the railed stairs.

Josie was on the stage, talking to a slim, dark-haired lady who wore an ankle-length blue dress and a fancy, wide-brimmed hat decorated with blue and lavender ribbons. At the sight of the women Lucky halted. Sarah proceeded toward the stage.

"I'm sorry I wasn't here when you came back," she said apologetically to Josie. "I went to see what the . . . what the town looked like."

Both women smiled patiently, obviously pleased she had decided to return at all.

"Sally, this is Miss Cashman," Josie said. "She has a hotel where you can stay, and the food there is very nice."

Sally saw kindness in the dark, gentle eyes of the woman who stood beside Josie. "But I have no money."

"We won't worry about money," Miss Cashman said. "Now tell me, Sally, have you no family in Tombstone?"

"No."

"Do your parents know where you are?"

"No. . . ." Sarah answered hesitantly, because she couldn't explain how she got here and didn't want to be asked. It would hardly do to say, *All this, including you, is just a dream . . . just make-believe.*

To her relief, no one asked. Miss Cashman probably meant to quiz her sometime, but chose not to do it now.

"You can come with me, Sally dear." She had an odd, pretty accent. Her smile was confident as she approached. "Who is your young friend? A relative?"

When Sally turned toward the railing where Lucky had been standing, she saw nothing there but the stage props. He had quietly slipped back down the stairs, probably not wanting to talk to the women. His exit didn't surprise her, especially considering the fact that just outside was tethered—a horse he had borrowed without permission. An awful feeling of aloneness gripped her.

He won't know where I am, she thought desperately. *He won't be able to find me.* Sally trembled. While she understood little of what was happening, she did know that she had fallen in love.

She might never see him again. Wasn't that how it often worked in dreams? Yet this...Somehow this was not a dream. She really was here in a scary frontier town, the way it was almost a hundred years ago. And Lucky had disappeared.

2

THE SHADOWS closed in on her. There was no electricity, only a kerosene lamp Miss Cashman had lighted, which Sally did not know how to put out. She sat in a borrowed white cotton nightgown that was much too large, staring at the floral patterns of the paper that lined all four walls of the little room.

Shivering, she asked herself over and over what she was going to do. It was awful here...in this town...in this time. She wanted her grandmother's warm, familiar house again, and her mother's sweet voice telling her it was all just her imagination. Most of all she wanted to see Lucky. Where was he?

Too exhausted to stay awake, she dozed in the strange bed until something—a knocking—woke her. Her heart began to pound with fear as she returned to full consciousness. She slid from the bed and crept toward the door. "Who is it?"

"Me!" the muffled voice said.

"Lucky?" She opened the door, and he quickly ducked inside.

"How did you find me?"

"Everyone knows where Nellie Cashman's hotel is. I snuck around and listened to her talking to her helper till I found out which was your room. Honest, I wasn't going to come till morning. I was trying to sleep on the straw at the OK Corral stables—that's where I slept last night—but somebody tried to steal my gun off me when I was starting to fall asleep. All the bars are open and drunks are all over the street! Drunks and bad women. I even heard some gunshots. It's fun watching all the people, but they stay up all night and I got tired. It must be way after midnight."

"It's the middle of the night. You can stay here and sleep. No one will know. Did you get dinner?"

"Yeah, I bought a steak." He unfastened his gun belt and set it carefully upon the table.

"You've been here by yourself without any money for two days?" she asked. "How come you're staying in town instead of going back home?"

"It's far," he said vaguely.

The strange look in his eyes told her it was not as simple as that. He didn't want to go home and didn't want to tell her why. Maybe his folks were mean and he had run away. Like Josie. The way Josie talked, this town must have a lot of runaways. Strange how they had happened to meet, she reflected. Lucky might be just as lost as she was.

It was cold, standing in the cotton gown and bare feet. Without a word she crawled back into the high, soft bed and watched her young cowboy struggle out of his boots, then clean himself with water from the pitcher on the washstand. He got into bed beside her.

"Thanks for letting me stay here," he mumbled sleepily.

"I'm your friend."

"My girlfriend. Will you be my girl?"

Her heart fluttered the strange way it had done when she first saw him standing in the theater.

This handsome, mysterious cowboy was her first boyfriend. Her first love. "Yes, I'll be your girl," she whispered happily.

He leaned over and softly kissed her cheek. In moments she heard his breathing change to a contented, even rhythm and knew he was asleep. He had kissed her! Well, at least her cheek. Feeling his closeness, Sally wanted to be at his side forever. To love and be loved was the best thing she'd ever known.

She was startled awake by a woman's voice. Light was shining in from the window. Nellie Cashman was standing beside her bed, smiling down.

Sally sat up. She was alone in the bed. Lucky was gone. He must have wakened early and left before he could be discovered. Thank heaven. How would she have explained his being there?

"We must go shopping today," the woman said. "To buy you a proper dress and some stockings."

"I don't want a dress," she protested. *Nor those hideous black stockings everyone wears.*

"We'll talk about it afterward. There's a hot breakfast waiting for you."

"I want to go back to the Bird Cage Theater this morning."

"You mustn't, dear. That is not a place for a young lady."

"Josie is there."

"Josie is an adult."

"She's not that much older than me!"

The woman gently pushed back the hair from Sally's face. "Josie's nineteen."

"And married?"

"I don't know."

Sally squeezed the pillow. "I have to go back there. I left something."

"We'll talk about it. Perhaps I can send someone for your things." Nellie smoothed the white apron she wore. "Now. You know where to find water for washing. I'll see you in the dining room. We'll have a nice conversation."

I don't want to have a nice conversation! Sally thought, panicking. *I don't know what to say.* She stretched her arms above her head. "What time is it?"

"Quite late. Nearly eight. You must have been very tired."

She nodded. The last things she remembered were the softness of Lucky's lips on her cheek and the warmth of his shoulder touching hers. She wondered where he was and what he was doing. It would not do to have someone else go after the pair of birds she had hidden in the theater. It had been too awkward yesterday to take the birds out of hiding, but she had to get them today.

Breakfast could wait. Sally washed and dressed hurriedly. Bypassing the dining room, she made her way onto Fifth Street. Yesterday, walking to the hotel with her, Miss Cashman had avoided Allen Street and instead chosen a street called Toughnut.

Now Sally retraced their steps to find her way to the Bird Cage. She couldn't enter by the saloon door, so she would have to go through the alley. This early, the cowboys probably wouldn't be at the back poker table. Hopefully, there wouldn't be anyone on the stage, so she'd be able to retrieve her birds and get out without being seen.

She was approaching the alley when a group of children carrying schoolbooks blocked her path. Two boys began circling her like buzzards. All were staring and grinning, especially the three girls, who wore loose dresses to midcalf with black stockings and ugly boots.

"Boy or girl?" one of the boys taunted her.

"What kind of shoes are those?" asked the other. "Shoes from Hoptown?"

"Even Hoptown don't have strap-on shoes," the other said, laughing as he spoke.

"Leave me alone!" Sally demanded, trying not to let her fear sound in her voice.

"The schoolmaster won't allow girls dressed like boys," a girl in a bonnet said.

Josie and Miss Cashman had mentioned school yesterday. Surely they wouldn't try to make her go to school with these horrible kids! She wouldn't, that was all! She didn't belong here and she wouldn't go! Lucky didn't attend school.

"Leave me alone," Sarah said again, when the boys continued to circle her.

"Maybe she was captured by Cochise and escaped!"

"Yeah! Indian shoes!"

They blocked her way so she couldn't proceed down the street.

The biggest boy, who looked about twelve or thirteen, pointed across the street to the area of small shacks and boardinghouses. "She lives in the red-light district. I bet her mama lives over there." He moved closer and touched her hair threateningly.

Suddenly Lucky appeared. He ran toward the group of laughing children and pushed his way to Sarah's side.

"You better apologize!" he demanded of the largest boy.

"Oh, yeah? Who are you? You come from Sixth Street, too?"

Lucky's blue eyes blazed. He drew the gun from his holster. "I told you to apologize!"

A deathly silence fell over the little crowd. Both boys stepped back. Giving Sally a sidelong glance, the bully muttered, "Sorry."

"If you want to push somebody around," Lucky told him, "try pushing me! Nobody talks to my girl like that and gets away with it."

"I ain't got a gun!" the boy howled.

Lucky handed his gun to Sally. "Hold this," he said, and to the bully, "Okay. Now we're even! Come on! You're so tough, teasing a girl.... Let's see what a big man you really are!"

To Sally's horror, the bigger boy accepted the challenge. The excited children formed a circle and a vicious fight began. It was obvious from the start the bully had no chance against Lucky, who fought as though he had been trained, coolly and controlled, dodging the flailing fists and landing every one of his blows solidly.

In the heat of the beating, the bully's companion produced a knife and moved in just long enough to get it into the hand of Lucky's opponent. The boy ducked away from a blow, reached out and stabbed Lucky's leg above the knee. The action was so fast that Sally scarcely realized what was happening until she saw the blade flash, and then blood soaking Lucky's jeans. He stumbled forward. She let out a shriek.

The children dispersed, taking off in two directions, leaving Sally and Lucky alone at the edge of the dusty street.

"I'll kill him!" Lucky groaned, sliding to the ground.

"He *stabbed* you! Oh, this is horrible! We have to find a doctor!"

"I don't want a doctor," he said. "Doctors ask too many questions." He was attempting to examine the wound, trying to tear his jeans away from the cut, but the denim was too strong to rip.

Sally, not wanting to hold the gun any longer, slid it back into his holster. "But what shall we do? Can you make it across to the back door of the theater? If Josie is there, she'll help us."

"Okay," he agreed. "I can't stay here."

The commotion had caught the attention of a cowboy standing at the corner. He approached them, looking down from the shade of his wide-brimmed hat. "Get yourself in a fight, did you, kid? How bad are you hurt?"

"He pulled a knife on me," Lucky answered. Sweat had formed on his forehead and his jaw was stiff.

"Doc Goodfellow is down the street."

"We were going into the Bird Cage," Sally told him, pointing to the back entrance.

The man raised his eyebrows and glanced at her curiously.

"We have a friend there."

"You sure?"

She nodded.

"All right, then. You'll never walk it, son. I'll give you a hand."

Lucky had no chance to protest. The powerfully built man then pulled the kerchief from his neck and placed it over the bleeding spot, scooped the boy up and carried him across the street and through the back door.

The dealer looked up and asked gruffly, impatiently, "What's going on?"

"Got a hurt kid," the cowboy replied without slowing his steps. He paused outside one of the two closed doors opposite the poker table. "Looks like these rooms are occupied."

The air was as tense as it was smoky around the card table. Chips were piled in mounds, card hands were facedown on the table, the squinting eyes of the players riveted on each other. It was obviously too important a moment for them to be bothered about a hurt kid. Chewing on his cigar, the dealer looked away.

"Go up to the stage," Sarah said, praying Josie would be there.

"I don't know about this, but I got to put you down somewhere." The tall cowboy climbed the stairs and laid his burden upon the hard cot that stood among the props. "You say you have a friend here? Who?"

"Her name is Josie."

"Little Josie Blue Eyes? Fancy that. I'd better find her for you. If she ain't here, she'll likely be over home, across the street." He leaned over the boy, produced a knife, and cut a section of his jeans away to expose the wound, then scowled. "You better let me get Doc Good-fellow."

"No. It's only a cut."

The cowboy shrugged. "Worried about getting in trouble, are you? Okay. I'll get Josie over here and let her talk some sense into you." He pulled aside the curtain and exited down the front steps of the stage into the dance hall.

Sarah took a peek at the wound. "This looks awful," she said, wincing. "It must really hurt!"

"Yeah, it does. I'm gonna find that kid and kill him."

"Not today, you're not."

Josie must have been in the saloon, because in moments she came running, carrying some bar towels.

"What on earth? Jess Hawks told me a boy was stabbed! Sally! What happened?"

"My friend was in a fight and the other kid pulled a knife on him."

She knelt beside the cot. "I saw you yesterday with Sally. What was the fight about?" She dabbed the blood with a towel and examined the wound. "Oh never mind, it doesn't matter." Her blond curls, worn loose this morning, bobbed about her face. "This will need stitches. Where are your parents?"

Lucky didn't answer. By now he had begun to tremble with the pain.

"Does your family know where you are?"

"No," he answered.

"I see. Another runaway. So you two are together. And in some kind of trouble. Jess said you don't want a doctor."

"No. No doctor." Lucky leaned forward and examined the wound himself as Josie wiped away the blood. "It doesn't look that deep to me." His face was very white and his hands shook.

Sarah thought, *He's in serious trouble of some kind. Why else would he want a gun? Why else would he not want to take a chance of his parents finding him?*

Josie said, "Sally, go down and ask the bartender for some clean cloths and a pair of scissors and a bottle of..." She stood up. "No, you can't do that. I'll go." She looked at Lucky. "You're right, the wound isn't terribly deep, but it is jagged and it has to be closed." She smoothed her skirt and gazed from one youngster to the other with the sad expression Sally had seen before. "Lord knows, I understand better than most what it is to be in trouble. I won't give you kids away. I'll stitch this cut myself."

Sally's stomach churned. "You mean with a needle?"

Josie smiled. "It's not the first wound I've ever stitched, pet, and I doubt if it'll be the last."

They heard her boot heels click on the steps then on the wooden floor. Voices and laughter wafted the length of the nearly empty theater.

Sarah knelt beside him again. "Lucky, you should have a doctor!"

He lay back on the narrow cot. "I've seen my dad stitch up a horse that got into barbed wire. It's like sewing up a torn shirt. She can do it as good as a doctor could."

I have to be brave like him, Sarah told herself fiercely, her fists clenched tight. *I can't be chicken now.* Forcing herself to ignore the queasiness of her stomach, she held a towel over the wound.

Lucky fell silent. His eyes closed, his jaw tight, she knew how scared he must be, but also knew he would never admit it.

Josie returned with a woman in a red and black dress who wore dark rouge and lipstick. They were carrying saloon serving baskets filled with towels and water and a bottle of whiskey.

"This is Pearl," Josie said, approaching the cot. "I didn't hear your name."

"Lucky," he answered.

"Not too appropriate this morning, is it?" She set down the basket, took out a pair of scissors and began cutting off the leg of his jeans.

Pearl handed him the whiskey. "Drink some down, kid. It'll numb your senses."

Sarah expected to be asked to stand aside while the adults set about their ministrations, but she wasn't. It was becoming obvious to her that children in the old West were treated differently. Eleven wasn't considered that young; no one had said a word about a kid having a gun. There was more concern about her being in a place where sin was going on than about protecting her from the more violent realities of life. She'd realized by now that Josie and Pearl were prostitutes, and knew what that word meant, yet it was still too abstract. Josie was a woman, but this morning, without her bright lipstick and blue eye shadow, she looked as young as some of the high school kids who hung around the Los Angeles malls.

What mattered was that Josie was a friend. She had given Sarah the bird she must have treasured. And now she was helping a boy she didn't know.

Lucky was drinking steadily now. At the first swallow he had made a terrible face and sputtered, but now the liquor seemed to be going down easier. Pearl was carefully washing the area around the wound and Josie had produced a needle and thread.

"Try to hold still," she said to her young patient. "Lean steady on his leg, Pearl, and blot the blood so I can see. Sally, give him your hands to hold on to. This will hurt a little, my lad, but don't worry, I know what I'm doing."

Lucky gritted his teeth and held Sally's hands tightly. He didn't cry, not one tear, but Sally's eyes were moist and hot and her limbs felt almost numb.

When it was over, Josie produced a blanket and a pillow and told him to try to sleep. "You'll have a scar as a souvenir," she said. "Look at this, Sally! Darned if the stitches don't form the shape of an L! You've got your initial carved forever on your leg, kid."

Groggy from the liquor and the pain, he closed his eyes.

The poker players' gruff voices could be heard below the stage now, and laughter from the saloon, but there was little activity in the theater proper because it was morning.

Josie said, "The next shift of miners won't get off work for another three hours, so it should be fairly quiet in here until then. But when their shift hits the place, they'll be demanding some entertainment."

Pearl looked at their patient. "Lucky won't want to move in any three hours, I'm sure of that. We can put him at the very back and pull down one of the backdrop curtains and no one will be any the wiser. He can sleep off his hangover all day."

"Good, we'll do that then." Josie smiled at Lucky. "But we won't move you yet, okay?"

He merely nodded. Sarah remembered that Miss Cashman would be looking for her, but it didn't matter. Nothing mattered, except staying by the side of the boy she loved, who needed her. He was enduring all this because he had come to her rescue and defended her honor.

"Can you sleep?" she asked him when they were finally alone.

"I don't know," he mumbled. "I feel very dizzy.... I think I'm drunk...."

She pulled a small stool to the side of the bed. "I won't leave you. Don't worry. I'm not going to leave."

His eyes were closed, but he wasn't sleeping. Still breathing fast, he was perspiring from the pain.

The women gathered up their makeshift surgical supplies. Josie drew back the front curtain at the top of the stage stairs, then stepped back quickly.

"What's wrong?" Pearl asked.

"I thought I saw him out there." Josie's voice trembled.

"Who? Your husband?" Pearl opened the curtain. The bar was filled with at least three dozen men. "Where? Which one?"

The color had drained from Josie's face. Watching from across the stage, Sarah felt her fear.

"I don't see him now. Maybe it was just my imagination. I saw a guy who looked like him from the back. I guess I panicked." She had dropped onto a red chair with a curved back. "He intends to kill me. He was going to follow me to Tombstone and kill me for leaving him."

"Go to the sheriff," Pearl said.

Josie laughed bitterly. "What makes you think the law would protect me? When Charlie tells them I'm his wife and I ran out, they'll just agree that he owns me."

Lucky opened his eyes and looked groggily at Sarah. They exchanged concerned looks.

"Josie is in awful danger," she whispered.

"And nobody to help her," he muttered. "'Cept me. When that Charlie guy shows up, I'll get him before he gets Josie."

Her eyes grew wide. She leaned closer. "You mean *shoot* him?"

He was perspiring badly, and it was clearly an effort for him to talk. His eyes kept closing, then he would force them open again. "It's better he gets shot than Josie."

"But . . . but would you really do it?"

"I'm a good shot." The blue eyes closed again. "Josie is our friend. I'm not gonna let anybody kill her. As soon as he shows up, I'll get him."

Sarah couldn't believe what she was hearing. "You'd go to jail for it!"

He smiled weakly. "I don't aim to shoot him in the back, Sally. Men don't go to jail for an honest fight in Tombstone."

The two women had moved off the stage and hadn't heard the whispered vow of Josie's new protector. Frightened, Sally leaned close to him. "You wouldn't actually have a . . . one of those gunfights? You're just a kid!"

"I told you, I'm a good shot. And I'm fast. Hardly anybody can outdraw me."

Maybe he's delirious, Sally thought. *Maybe he's drunk.* It did no good, though, to try to convince herself he didn't have every intention of carrying out his threat.

Lucky lay still, his eyes closed again, and the sounds of the saloon at the far end of the theater seemed very far away. The stage was eerily silent. For uncounted minutes Sarah studied his face, marveling at the beauty of him and thinking of his bravery. He had fought for *her*. For the first time in her young life, she was truly and deeply in love.

As if he had read her mind, Lucky opened his eyes. In the soft light they looked misty and very blue. "You're the prettiest girl I ever saw...."

She bent down and kissed him gently.

"I love you," he whispered.

"I love you, too."

Smoothing his damp hair from his forehead, Sally smiled. "Just one minute. I'll be right back."

The ornamental birds were in their hiding place. Unwrapping the green silk scarf that protected them, she crossed the stage and sat down beside him again.

"I have two glass birds that are very, very old," she whispered. "I think they are magical. The birds are a pair and the magic can happen only when they are together. I'm going t'give one to you and I'll keep the other. That way the birds will always stay together... always... like you and me."

She placed one of the birds in his hand, and he glanced at her quizzically.

"They're a pair," she repeated. Gently, Sally touched their wings together.

Suddenly the room went dark. She felt a swirl of strange dizziness.

Then there was light again, and she was in the attic of her grandmother's home, holding one glass bird. The stage and Lucky were gone.

"Lucky!" she shrieked. "No! Come back!"

Tears streaming down her cheeks, she gazed at the bird in her hand. Its wings were not streaked with pink and yellow like the one she had found in her grandmother's trunk. This was the bird Josie had given her! Lucky had the other!

"Don't go!" she pleaded. "Don't go away! I love you!"

Sarah slumped onto the floor and buried her face in her arms. The memories were so vivid that she could still feel the warmth of his hands in hers. Her heart ached, and a new and devastating pain enveloped her. *Where was he?*

"Lucky! I'll always love you," she sobbed. "Always . . . always . . . always. . . ."

But only the shadows could hear. The shadows and the solitary glass bird she was clutching in her hand.

From the attic stairs came familiar voices, those of her mother and father. The voices sounded frantic.

Sally walked shakily to the top of the steps. Her mother shrieked and rushed to embrace her. "Where have you been, Sally? Where have you been for the last twenty-four hours?"

3

A HUNDRED YEARS hadn't silenced the ghosts. Twenty years hadn't dimmed the memories.

Now, on the day before her thirty-first birthday, Sarah stood once again in the Bird Cage Theater, feeling as if it were all a dream. The voices of other tourists faded into the echo of Josie's voice, into the sound of Lucky's breathing, the last thing she had heard here twenty years ago. The incredible dream was alive again.

The tears in her eyes glazed away the dust and scars of time and polished everything with the fresh mist of memory. The sensation that she had only to turn around to see him was overpowering. Suddenly numb, Sarah walked under the fourteen overhead cages and climbed the worn steps onto the stage.

The voices in her head grew stronger, the pain in her chest almost intolerable. She had missed him so! Even now, after twenty years, she missed him. A few museum relics were on display here—furniture and a hearse that had been once horse drawn—an ominous reminder that Lucky could no longer be alive. Standing on the spot where he had lain, she heard him say again, "I love you," and thought her heart would break.

It wasn't a dream. Through the years she had tried to convince herself it was, even though she'd always known better. Her family had accused her of running away because she hadn't been in the attic, or anywhere else, that late afternoon when they'd looked for her. When she had tried to talk to her mother about Tombstone, she'd been told she'd had a nightmare, a nightmare she deserved for worrying everyone and running off to the woods without a word. They'd assumed she had lost her way home when it grew dark. Sometimes, Sarah herself believed this. Except when the bright, vivid memories returned. Now she knew she had not been in the woods near her grandmother's house on the night of her eleventh birthday. She had been at Nellie Cashman's hotel, sleeping beside the boy she loved.

For twenty years she'd been haunted by her dream. She'd fantasized often about coming to Tombstone, but put it off "until a more convenient time" when she wasn't so busy. In reality she'd been afraid to face the truth.

And being busy had been an easy excuse. After completing college and a master's degree in media studies, she had launched a career as a screenwriter while working as a camera assistant in a television studio. But a book on old Tombstone, Arizona, and its history had always been by the side of her bed. The history of the silver-mining days was as much a part of her life as the memories of her own childhood. Among her most treasured possessions was a book with a photo of the interior of the Bird Cage Saloon, a book she had checked out of the public library a long, long time ago and pretended to lose; she'd paid the book fine with her meager twelve-year-old's allowance.

"Someday I'll go," she'd told herself on a regular basis, but whenever she said it, her stomach would constrict with fear. How could she go, knowing Lucky wasn't there? The truth was, she only wanted to remember it as a dream.

Until now. She had assumed that enough time had gone by, but it hadn't; the pain was still too sharp. Nevertheless, beyond the ever-needling curiosity, she had a reason for being here now.

The screenplay.

All the emotion, all the joy, the sadness, and most of all, her firsthand knowledge of the early days, was going into that play, her first major venture on her own. She wanted to write, not about Lucky, but about Josie. About Josie's life as a prostitute in a mining town. Had she survived the visit from her husband? Sarah had wondered a thousand times. Had Lucky really gotten himself involved, as he'd sworn he would after Josie stitched his leg?

Had he killed a man for Josie? Had he been killed for her? In the screenplay Josie would survive the husband, but not the life-style of a saloon whore.

To her left was the backstage stairway Lucky had led her down. The stairway he had been carried up with a bleeding leg. Standing at the same railing, Sarah looked down to the level below. To her surprise, the poker table and chairs were still there, cards and cigars on the table as if the somber, mustached players would return any minute.

Who could have imagined the place would be so well preserved? It was absolutely eerie. What had changed, though, was the air. There was no cigar smoke now or the stench of whiskey; the air was stale with mildew and alive with the vibrations of the ghosts. She could feel their cold, restless presence trying to capture her, to pull her back with them.

She was almost choking. Sarah had to get out. Lucky was still with her, leading her away as he had done the day she met him.

Outside there were changes. Where the cribs and boardinghouses of the red-light district had been, now stood school buildings and a tennis court. Just around the corner, across from an open area, was the spot where the fight had taken place, where Lucky had been stabbed. Sarah dared not close her eyes for fear of seeing it all again . . . the blood, the pain in his eyes. . . .

It's too real! she screamed inside herself, trembling, retracing their steps down Allen Street, along the wooden sidewalks and past the rustic storefronts, behind which were now souvenir shops. The Crystal Palace Saloon was still there, but most of the others were gone. All the same, that mildewed air was strangely sinister, somehow laced with evil.

Toughnut Street was still here, and to her surprise, so was Nellie Cashman's hotel. Now it was a restaurant. Up on the hill were the silent mounds of once-thriving mining operations.

Fremont Street. The millinery store and gun shops were gone.

The loneliness was intense, but she wasn't supposed to be alone here. To her embarrassment, Sarah found herself looking at the faces of young boys, almost expecting to find Lucky's face, Lucky's smile. Lucky's clear blue eyes.

The February dusk was beginning to fall and the streets were growing deserted as the air cooled. She looked at her watch. For nearly two hours she had been wandering about, lost in a dream. The motel would not hold her reservation past six.

Driving toward the edge of town, she found the rugged silhouettes of the distant Dragoon Mountains hauntingly familiar. When she'd last been here, Apache warriors sometimes rode down, spears in hand, and left death in their wake.

Checking into the motel, she told the desk clerk, "I'll be staying about a week, I think. I want to research the early history of Tombstone."

"The courthouse has been converted into a historical museum," the man told her. "You might start there."

Sarah nodded. "I'd like to find a historian who would agree to talk to me. It's for a film project."

The man smiled, handed her a room key and scratched his gray head. "I'll give you the name of a guy who knows as much about the history of the boom days as anybody else alive. Friend of mine. He'd be the one to talk to."

Perfect. An old-timer, she thought, returning her credit card to her billfold. "Is there a number where he can be reached?"

"Sure. He doesn't live in town, though. He owns the Verde Springs Ranch over west a few miles. It's the ranch his great-great-granddad founded in the days of the Indian raids." The clerk scribbled a name and number on the back of a motel business card and handed it to her.

She read the name. "Scott MacInnes. Thanks. I'll give him a call."

In her room, Sarah immediately dialed the number. A woman's voice answered. After she asked for Mr. MacInnes, it was nearly two full minutes before he picked up the phone."

"Scott here." The voice was deep and pleasant and did not sound like that of an old-timer.

"Mr. MacInnes, my name is Sarah Christianson. I've just arrived in Tombstone to do research for a film script on the boom days, and I've been told you are an expert historian. I wonder if you would agree to an interview. I'll make sure you get credit on the screen."

"Sure," the deep voice answered. "Why not? I'm not interested in credit for serving up a small plate of local history, though."

"I'm . . . sorry if I disturbed you. Were you outside?"

"Yeah, just came in. Do you want to drive out to the ranch?"

"That would be super. When is convenient?"

"Evenings. Come on out now, if you like. I plan to throw a steak on the barbecue after I get a shower. I can cook two as easily as one, and open another beer."

"That's awfully kind...."

"My pleasure. I'm out twenty-four miles on Highway 82. You catch it north of Boot Hill Cemetery. Just look for a gate with a Verde Springs sign. I'll see you in—what? About an hour?"

"I'll be there."

Twenty-four miles, and people acted as if it wasn't any distance at all. Maybe it wasn't, by local standards. Sarah unpacked quickly, carefully lifting her antique glass bird from the padded box where she had kept it safe. She set it upon the table by the bed. "You're home," she told the silent, mysterious little bird.

FALLING DARKNESS hid some of the scenery as she drove west. A few miles out, the terrain changed drastically. Dry, thorny, cactus-choked land gave way to gentle, grass-covered hills darkened by the spiny silhouettes of scattered yuccas. Then the yuccas were gone and in their place stood patches of scrub oaks. Shadows moved in the twilight breezes over open areas of prairie grass.

The Verde Springs sign was easy to spot; it hung from an arch of varnished wood over a narrow road that forked off the highway. She followed the side road for another half mile until she saw the lights of a rambling, white-stuccoed ranch house and what seemed like miles of low, white fences. Branches of huge cottonwoods grew so thickly overhead that the approaching night appeared to descend all at once; the air darkened from gray to black.

A floodlight brightened the path from the driveway to the front door. The night was cool and unnervingly quiet. Quiet beyond anything she had ever experienced or even imagined, growing up in the Los Angeles area. A half moon hung low in the sky and stars were beginning to sparkle. From somewhere the barking of a dog broke the stillness. Sarah stepped onto a porch where plants grew in profusion in huge clay pots. She pulled the bell on a heavy, carved door.

The voice on the phone had been deep, educated, friendly and not old. What she expected Scott MacInnes to look like, Sarah wasn't sure, but the man who opened the door and stood half in shadow with the soft light from the interior behind him, was such a surprise that she stepped back involuntarily.

He stood well over six feet and his shoulders were nearly as broad as the doorway. As her eyes adjusted to the light, the handsome features of his face and his sky-blue eyes came into focus. There was something about him that caused a flash of dizziness, but perhaps it was just the startling appearance of such an attractive man when she'd expected a studious historian. The rancher looked like a poster cowboy in his tight jeans and boots, muscles bulging from the shirtsleeves rolled up to his elbows.

"I'm Sarah Christianson," she introduced herself.

He held out his hand. "Scott MacInnes. Come in."

"It's lovely here, Mr. MacInnes. I've never been on a ranch in my life. I had no idea how quiet the country is at night."

"City people sometimes find the silence unnerving." He smiled.

His smile was enchanting and reminded her of someone, but she couldn't think who.

"Personally," he continued, "I find the country a great relief from Tombstone. The town is quiet, too, in its own way, but in the dead of night the feeling of being surrounded by the ghosts is damned distracting. Come on through to the back. I'll check the charcoal."

I'm not the only one who feels the presence of the ghosts, she thought, following him through a room with brightly colored Navajo rugs hung on the walls and more Indian rugs scattered on the tile floors. The round fireplace that dominated one corner was decorated with Mexican tiles. The sparse furniture was massive and dark, probably Mexican, too.

"Your house is beautiful."

"This section is part of the original ranch house," he replied. "It looks pretty much as it did when my great-great-grandparents lived here."

There was no sign of anyone else. Where was the woman—his wife?—who had answered the phone? she wondered.

He stepped into a kitchen decorated with the same rustic tiles and low-beamed ceilings, and turned quizzical eyes upon her. Why was he looking at her like that?

"What will you have to drink?" he asked huskily.

"You mentioned beer."

"Right. Good. I'm ready for another myself." He took two cans and two chilled mugs from the refrigerator, poured, and handed one to her.

A long hallway from the kitchen opened into the Arizona room, a spacious area with windows on all sides. There were no curtains, and the stars of the night sky were visible from all corners. In the center stood a round table and chairs; to one side was a grouping of leather casual chairs.

"I'll just check the grill outside," he said. "I hope you're hungry. How do you like your steak?"

"Medium." This was not the time to tell him it had been months since she'd eaten a steak. As a guest of a rancher, one didn't make an issue of wanting to eliminate red meat. "Do you barbecue every night?"

"More often than not. I like to give my housekeeper the evenings off, so I do my own cooking at night and the grill is the easiest. No kitchen mess."

"You're not married?"

"Nope. What about you?"

"No."

He grinned. "I hoped you'd say no. I feel more comfortable entertaining a single lady. After I hung up the phone, I realized I had taken it for granted you were alone. Glad I was right."

"It was kind of you to invite me."

"You wanted to talk about Tombstone's history. My favorite subject. Besides, I have a pretty good historical library you might want to look through."

The tiled patio was enclosed on three sides by the walls of the house itself. A brick barbecue had been built at the far end. Sarah watched him pick up tongs and lift out two foil-wrapped potatoes from under the coals, set them aside, and slap two large steaks onto the grill. He grimaced and blinked as smoke rose into his face. She took advantage of this distraction to study him. It wasn't every day one happened upon a man so beautiful to look at.

"It won't be long," he said.

"Can I help?"

"I don't like to put guests to work, but I guess you could get the salad bowl from the refrigerator. Rosa always prepares the salad because she knows I'm too lazy to make it. There are rolls in a basket on the kitchen counter."

Minutes later, they were seated across from each other in the soft light of candles.

"I realize this is casual bordering on crude," he said. "Can't help it. It's the way I live."

"I like the way you live." She smiled. "Is Verde Springs a large ranch? Hundreds of cattle?"

"Not even one head," he answered, serving her salad. "My father was a cattleman, but beef ranching isn't to my liking, and I sold the herds after Dad died. I breed and train quarter horses for a living." He served himself the remainder of the salad. "Now. Tell me about your writing project and what you need from me."

"I write screenplays," she answered. "Scripts for television. For three years I've been working as part of a team, and this is my first solo project. It's a story that takes place in Tombstone in the early 1880s. Experience has taught me that talking to experts is far better research than merely reading, because experts have so much to contribute on their own—their particular or peculiar interests, their life experiences." She raised her arm in a sweeping motion. "This, for instance . . . this atmosphere. Reading about a ranch in southern Arizona is hardly the same as being here, listening to the silence and looking at the vast night sky."

He nodded. "Your screenplay is fiction?"

"Yes, but the setting must be authentic."

Scott MacInnes didn't look especially pleased. "I see. You'll use the gunfight at the OK Corral—that sort of thing."

"No. Not gunfights. I'm particularly interested in the Bird Cage Theater. My characters are employed there as 'ladies of the evening.' I want to get as good an idea as possible of what their lives were like, and no books I've ever found were much help."

Now he looked even less pleased. Scott stared at her for a few seconds, then looked down and cut a bite of steak but didn't eat it. "Very little is known about them. Prostitutes rarely used last names, and even if they did, the names were probably false. It's impossible to trace their lives unless they were connected with someone famous, like Big Nose Kate, who was Doc Holliday's mistress before she was run out of town." He looked at her with a troubled expression. "Why prostitutes?"

"For one thing, the Bird Cage is fascinating. So much happened there. It could tell a thousand stories if its walls could talk."

"If its walls could talk, a great deal of what they said would be unprintable. The theater was a bordello with a reputation that went far beyond the boundaries of the Arizona Territory."

Sarah grinned. "Which is precisely what makes it such a great backdrop. I am amazed at how well preserved the old theater is."

"The owners closed the doors and let it sit untouched for fifty years."

"What foresight! I stepped in there for the first time today and walked around, imagining it as it was back then."

"Did you imagine all color and glamour? The actual lives of those 'fallen women' were hell. Hardly like a glamorized television movie."

Sarah's eyes met his. "Oh? You're so certain I would depict their lives as glamorous?"

"Wouldn't you?"

"Certainly not. There is nothing glamorous about prostitution in any circumstances. How the women coped with the degradation, though, how they survived, that interests me."

He concentrated for a moment on his food. "A lot of them didn't cope. They committed suicide or drank themselves to death. A very few did marry local cow-boys. I know of at least one—Irish Mag she was called—who grubstaked a prospector and the guy hit a rich silver vein. Mag sailed home to Ireland with half a million bucks." He popped a large bite into his mouth and chewed it, then continued. "A few of the more en-terprising gals later established bordellos of their own. All their backgrounds were murky and their futures unknown. They moved on to other boomtowns after the silver mines closed."

Sarah was uncomfortable with the tone of his voice. He spoke with a mixture of impatience and disdain.

He went on. "I can tell you a few stories and names of Tombstone's most notorious and pathetic ladies of joy, but beyond that, I'm not much good on this sub-ject. Ask me about the gunfighters and outlaws, and I promise to shine."

"But many 'ladies of the night' are well-known," Sarah argued, ignoring his almost threatening man-ner. Why was he trying to steer her off the subject of "fallen women"? "Like Crazy Horse Lil, Madam Mus-tache, Dutch Annie..."

"Known around town, yeah. But keep in mind that at one time there were thirty-seven hundred of them here. No one knew or cared where they came from or where they went. Hell, Sarah, no one cares now." He emptied his glass and rose. "Excuse me for a second. I'm going to get us another beer."

Thirty-seven hundred! She hadn't known that. *What did he mean, no one cares? I, for one, care.* Sarah set down her fork and looked out at the clear night sky. Stars were shining brightly. Earlier she had been able to see the outlines of corrals and other ranch buildings, but now a cloak of darkness covered the landscape. Her reflection and that of the burning candles were mirrored in the window glass. Sitting in the small circle of light in the candle-lit room brought on a sudden sensation of isolation, as if there were no other life around them, just this room.

Scott MacInnes seemed a charming and easygoing guy in some respects, but she was afraid he was not going to be as cooperative as she had first hoped. If her questions had been about the Earps and the other bloodthirsty gunfighters, they would be doing just fine. But she wanted to know about *women.* Worse, "fallen women." A subject he had just made clear he didn't care about.

Sarah picked unenthusiastically at her salad. *Discuss women? The least fortunate of women?* she muttered to herself. *When there are matters here that have to do with guns and drunken fights and mindless murder?* Hell, what could she expect from a cowboy? Lucky had had the same kind of macho mind-set; she remembered how scornfully he'd spoken of "bad women."

Scott returned with two cold cans of beer and refilled her glass, saying, "The 'soiled doves' had to buy licenses in order to practice their trade. You can find some of those licenses still on record but very few include surnames. Seven dollars a month, I think they paid." He picked up a roll. "I'm trying to be helpful here, Sarah, but hell, I assumed you would be asking about Doc Holliday and Johnny Ringo and the Earp brothers, like everybody else does."

"I know." Perhaps he didn't like the idea that she had brought up a subject on which he had less expertise. He sat across from her with an odious, why-on-earth-would-anyone-be-interested-in-prostitutes? expression in his penetrating blue eyes. Unnerving eyes.

Plainly defending his stance, he said, "Tombstone was the wildest frontier town in the American West. Not a few notorious characters headed down here when Dodge City ran them out. Rustler gangs moved back and forth across the Mexican border, and the Apaches were killing prospectors who wandered into the Dragoon Mountains. The sheriff was in cahoots with the outlaw gangs, and the Federal deputy marshals—Wyatt Earp and his brothers—were also accused of being murderers and criminals. Sheriff Behan and the marshals were archenemies even before Wyatt stole the sheriff's mistress. Murder was commonplace and rarely punished unless a man was shot in the back. Lots of good stories there, ma'am. You must have read the popular history."

"I have, yes. I'm trying to rout out details that are not generally known except by experts like yourself." She took a swallow of the beer. "Is it just a hobby, then, your deep interest in Tombstone's history?"

"Yeah. It's my heritage. My great-great-grandfather was among the first miners to arrive."

"He was a miner? From where? Tell me about him."

Scott pushed aside his plate, and the expression in his eyes softened. "Ian MacInnes was a Cornish Jack—that is, he was a mine worker as a lad in Britain. Knowing the business, he decided to prospect on his own, and when he made a rich strike, he put his money in land. As soon as the railroad reached Benson, ranching became a big business out here."

"So there is true pioneer blood in your veins," she said with a smile.

He returned the smile. Why was it so hauntingly familiar? The tension eased. "My mother was one of the territory's local historians. She got me involved when I was just a kid. I was Wyatt Earp in all my boyhood games and fantasies. Practiced with a six-shooter until I was good enough to win every local competition. Those gunfighters were my heroes, the way other kids have baseball heroes. I must have shot ten thousand tin cans full of bullet holes in my lifetime.

"Hell," Scott said. "I confess I still do it every now and then."

"Do what?"

"Practice my fast draw on tin cans." He grinned. "Men only pretend to grow up, Sarah. Most women know that, I suspect."

She laughed. At least he was admitting that a fascination with guns and shooting was not very adult. He wasn't killing himself trying to make an impression, which, of course, made the greatest impression of all.

Sarah wondered what he was thinking about her. She knew she was attractive to men. The way Scott Mac-

Innes gazed at her told her he liked what he saw—a
woman is never wrong about that—but it wasn't so
easy to gauge what he was thinking now. And he knew
that she, too, had been pleasantly shocked at the door;
he had the self-assurance of a man who was aware of
his own good looks. His every move was sensual; he
probably was aware of that, as well. And his gaze was
unnerving at the least expected times.

At this moment, for instance. The blue, blue eyes re-
flecting candlelight were fixed on her as though he were
hypnotized by something he saw in her face.

"What is it?" Sarah asked.

"What?"

"You're staring at me."

He blinked. "I'm sorry. I didn't mean to stare. Maybe
it's your laughter. Your laughter is so musical, like a
song I know."

"What song?"

"I don't remember. A song I've heard somewhere."

When he looked away, down at the table, it seemed
to Sarah as if the room suddenly grew darker because
she couldn't see his eyes.

4

SCOTT PUSHED his plate aside and leaned back in his chair. "So..." he began forcefully. "Tell me more about this writing project of yours."

She swallowed, fighting to keep from falling under the mysterious spell of his eyes. Damn, *this* had never happened to her before . . . well, only once before. She must be feeling the enchantment of Tombstone again, and an encounter with a man whose eyes were as intensely blue as Lucky's was too much stimulus.

Ignoring her strange feeling, Sarah answered, "I've outlined the plot and drafted the script. Now I need authenticity and the mood of the early 1880s."

"How much time have you given yourself to absorb the 'authenticity'?"

"Six weeks. I might decide to stay and finish writing the play here. Because this project is my first solo flight, it's important to me. It can represent a major step up in my career."

"And your characters are prostitutes."

"Two are. One was forced into prostitution when her husband left her, and the other ran away from an abusive childhood. I believe a great many of these women ran away from childhood abuse. They were victims of their time. Few professions were open to women on the

frontier. My characters are neither dishonest nor violent."

He scratched his chin. "I thought you were going for
authenticity."

"I am, Scott!"

"The good-hearted prostitute cliché? They lived on
the edge of the law and they were tough. They had to
be to survive."

She bristled, remembering Josie. On this matter the
"expert" knew less than she did.

"Are you saying you don't believe a dance-hall
woman was capable of kindness?"

He fell into a short, thoughtful silence. "I didn't say
that. There always are exceptions, but a good number
of these 'soiled doves' had criminal records for robbery, even murder. I'm only pointing out facts. You did
say you're interested in facts."

"Background facts, yes. My story itself is fiction."

He rubbed his chin again and leaned an elbow on the
table. His voice softened. "Why don't you write the
truth about the boom days of Tombstone? Lord knows,
it would be refreshing. There is so much junk, so many
legends are touted as truth. Lies told so many times
people think they're true."

Sarah sat back and studied Scott carefully; his attitude had begun to annoy her. He was discounting her
project and telling her to change it to something *he*
would find more palatable. Nevertheless she needed his
help, so it was to her advantage not to let him rattle her.

"You're very adamant," she said. "I see your point in wanting real history to prevail over myth, but I'm not a writer of history. I'm a storyteller."

Obviously a man accustomed to having things his way, Scott seemed bent on arguing. "What's wrong with telling true stories, then? Tombstone's history is wilder than any writer's imagination."

She pushed her hair back from her shoulders. "This is beginning to sound like an argument and I don't understand why. Why don't you want me to write about your hometown?"

Scott rose, walked to the window and stood with his back to her, looking into the darkness. "Maybe I have a hang-up. Just so much trash is being written. For those of us who know the facts, it gets very tiresome. Tourists come because of the Western films. They come from Germany and Japan and Australia, all to have a look at the OK Corral and imagine the gunfight. Only it actually took place a block away. They want to walk in Wyatt Earp's footsteps. They buy stupid souvenirs. It's all commercialized."

"How could it not be now? If the gunfight was a block away, what real difference does it make?" Glad she had done her homework, Sarah said, "I understand what you're saying, though. My script is commercial, too. It may be fiction, but it represents a time in history and a way of life. What's wrong with that? I'm interested in ordinary people who might have been there, not your infamous gun-fighting 'heroes.' And anyway, they weren't really heroes, they were thugs."

He turned to look at her. "Thugs?"

"Precisely. As a historian, you have to know what they were."

"Lawmen of the frontier." His tone was light, even amused.

"Thugs."

"That's a rude word, Sarah."

She couldn't tell whether he was offended or just playing along, because there was so much mischief in his eyes. "Lawmen? Sure! I thought you were so hung up on the truth."

"I am," he said. "Which do *you* want, though? Truth or fiction? I suppose I can give you either one."

This was ridiculous. They were going around in circles, and she wasn't sure what they were arguing about, except that he didn't like her insulting his heroes and sympathizing with whores. Of all the stupid things! It wasn't as if some of his gun-toting heroes hadn't fallen in love with these same women.

Scott MacInnes had to be one of the most opinionated human beings she'd ever met. One would think she was writing about his contemporaries, the way he was carrying on.

"I have the impression you have only contempt for my creative project, and that's grossly unfair. I'm good at what I do, and the script has real potential. A reasonable person wouldn't interfere with the artist's basic concept."

"People believe what they see on television," Scott responded. "Your film, with its so-called authentic background, will be mistaken for actual history."

"It will not."

"It will, and you know it."

She gestured, feeling helpless. "Look, Scott, I know you're a busy man. I don't want to impose on your time."

He bent to pick up a large desert tortoise that was sauntering toward them. Then he sprawled onto one of the leather chairs, one ankle over the other knee, holding the heavy animal on his chest and scratching its leathery chin. Sarah watched all this, fascinated. The tortoise was plainly a pet he was very fond of.

Temporarily disarmed, Sarah pondered. What was it that bothered her so much?

The short silence seemed to have warmed the atmosphere. "I thought you wanted the best history source you can get," he said mildly.

"Of course I do."

"That would be me. If you're interested in the 1880s in the Territory, I know things nobody else does."

That was an odd boast. She squinted at him. "How could you?"

"Just take my word for it. I've known people who were there."

So have I! Sarah wanted to shout, but couldn't. There was no way to explain that she had been in 1882. What she needed from him were local stories, less-known facts, and the ability to separate fact from myth. "Does that mean you're willing to talk to me, even though you aren't keen on my subject?"

"I gave my word. I'm honor bound." The contented tortoise still lying on his chest, he looked up and smiled. "Anyway, it might be interesting delving into stuff about the 'fallen angles' of Allen Street."

"If it makes you feel any better, I'll include a gun-fight outside the Bird Cage—as background only, though." Sarah looked at her watch. "I've had a very long day. Could we meet again tomorrow? I could buy you dinner in town."

"There's more peace and privacy out here," Scott answered. "Why don't you come out at your convenience tomorrow and use my library? You won't find a better one. Bring your swimsuit and take a dip in the pool. It's heated. Then, when I finish my work, we'll have a bite of dinner, a bottle of good wine, and talk like two serious adults."

"Adults," she repeated. "All right. I'd love to come out. Will you be working with your horses tomorrow?"

"Yes. You can make yourself at home." He struggled to his feet, gently setting the tortoise on the floor. "Come on, I'll show you where the library is. I'll probably be out when you get here. I'll have Rosa prepare lunch for you. In fact, I think I'll ask her to make us some of her terrific tamales for dinner, if that suits you."

"You're a gracious host. Thank you."

They walked into the newer area of the house. The library was a wood-paneled room lined with bookshelves and well lit. Two reclining chairs flanked a table in the center.

"I try to keep my books in some kind of order," he said. "Otherwise I could never find anything. Right through here are volumes on the history of the Arizona Territory. Most of them I inherited from my mother. A few I've procured myself."

Sarah turned and eagerly began studying titles.

"There isn't a lot on prostitutes," he added. "Nobody has known enough about them to write much."

"Or cared enough to find out, as you said. Who did you know from the boom days?"

"A few old characters. All dead now."

"Mmm. Do you know much about Nellie Cashman?"

"The Angel of Tombstone? Sure. All the information that's known about her is here. Jot down any questions you have and we'll discuss them."

"You're more than kind. Do you do this for everyone?"

"No. But it isn't every day someone like you knocks on my door—someone whose laugh reminds me of a song I can't quite remember. Maybe I'll remember it tomorrow."

They returned to the front foyer and she asked, "Are you going to try to change my mind about my script's focus?"

"Absolutely. What's written about my town is important to me, whether I ever see the film or not. I never watch television."

"That's what everybody says. But everybody watches it."

He smiled again and walked her to her car. The night was crisp. A coyote howled in the distance. And nearer, a horse softly neighed. Two tail-wagging dogs bounded out of the shadows and frolicked around their master.

"It's beautiful out here," she said, as much to herself as to anyone else.

"Beauty appreciates beauty. So do I. I'm glad I've made your acquaintance, Miss Christianson. Watch for coyotes on the road."

"Till tomorrow, then," Sarah said from inside her car.

HE STAYED OUTSIDE with his dogs until he could no longer see her headlights. The night closed in around him; years closed in around him. A hundred years.

A century ago it was the same sky. The same grove of trees behind the house. The coyotes prowled the hills then, as now, and howled at the moon on still, deep nights. But a century ago there'd been Apache war parties not far away and gangs of rustlers moving along the ridges in the darkness.

He remembered it very well.

He should have stayed in that time, Scott thought; he'd been meant to live then. The girl he'd loved had needed him and he'd left her. What had become of her? And what had she thought when she'd found him gone?

Scott MacInnes had asked himself these questions a thousand times in the past two decades, but never found the answers. Nor had he ever found another girl like her. Now he knew he never would. He was destined to be alone, caught in limbo with memories that had such a hold on his life that he could never free himself from them.

Strange how he'd loved her so easily, so completely. What was stranger still, he'd never loved since. Even now, approaching his thirty-first birthday, he wanted no one but the beautiful girl who had lived and died long ago. The girl who had loved him.

1882. He could taste the dust of that year. He could hear its sound: horses' hooves on the wide, dirt streets; music from the dance halls; gunshots in the darkness. He could breathe its smell: spilled whiskey; gunpowder; cheap perfume; straw-filled stables. He could feel the air of 1882 in his lungs. But he could never be there again.

He had tried to return to her. Tried everything. His heart and soul and mind were caught and captured in a world he could not reach again, even though 1882 was where he belonged. He should have grown up to make his own mark upon the history of the Town Too Tough to Die. He would have held his own against rustlers, carved out his own reputation. But he could never get back.

Kneeling under the stars of the February night, petting his dogs, Scott had once again lost himself in his memories. Spending tonight with Sarah Christianson had brought back the memories even more vividly, more poignantly than usual. His chest was burning, his eyes ached. Damn her, bringing back the past like that!

Maybe he had made a mistake in inviting her out to-morrow. He must have been carried away by her beauty—and by the strange effect she'd had on him.

The dogs followed at his heels. They begged for scraps while he cleaned up the grill and piled the rinsed dishes in the sink. What had happened tonight? He still couldn't figure it out.

Something about that woman was driving him crazy, making him restless as hell. The discomfort had begun the moment she walked in. It wasn't just her soft blue eyes and golden hair. It was something else, a strong sense of something right and something wrong all mixed together. And when she laughed . . .

Tonight the memories punched hard, causing the same pain in his stomach he used to feel as a boy. In those days he would down a handful of aspirin and go out to target practice, but in the end he'd always had to lie down in the grass and simply surrender to the pain of remembering. He'd lain under the clouds and sworn he'd find his way back to Sally's world, then wondered why it hurt so much to remember her.

Tonight the same pain gnawed inside him, and he felt the confinement of the house. He couldn't go target-practicing in the dark, but he could ride. He saddled his favorite mare and cantered down the long training runs, wishing it were light enough to take off across the hills.

His memories outran him. The wind moaning in the trees reminded him of the same sad song as Sarah's laughter had.

Her laughter haunted him. He gazed into the darkness. *Who was the woman who had walked into his life tonight?*

5

SARAH TOSSED AND TURNED. Thoughts of Scott Mac-
Innes crawled across her mind like spiders spinning
webs—back and forth, in circles. The thoughts grew
hopelessly tangled, then blurred. She wasn't normally
combative, but he bothered her. Secrets were locked
away somewhere behind his puzzling blue eyes. She was
almost afraid to look into them because when she did,
she saw someone very different from the person she
thought she was. It frightened her. It was almost as if
he were looking at her and seeing someone else.

Drifting into a shallow sleep, she dreamed of Lucky.
In the dream his eyes were too deep to see into and his
hands were those of Scott MacInnes, holding a huge
desert tortoise. Why Scott's hands?

Of course I would dream about Lucky, she told herself when she awoke. *I'm in Tombstone again.* Lucky
had been on her mind ever since she'd got here. Sigh-
ing in the dark room, Sarah wished she had finished her
job. Walking alone on the streets where she had walked
with him was too hard, too sad.

SHE REACHED the Verde Springs Ranch at ten-thirty.
Driving up, she could see him working with a horse in

silhouette, in a distant field. He waved and she waved back, surprised that he had seen her.

Everything looked different in daylight. White buildings with red tile roofs. Large areas planted with bright green winter grass. A big swimming pool sparkled in the sunlight. There had to be money in raising quarter horses.

Rosa, in jeans and a sweatshirt, opened the door with a pleasant smile. She offered coffee and brought a pot of it to the library with a tray of cinnamon tortillas.

Even surrounded by Scott's private world, it was easy for Sarah to lose herself in the history books when everything she read reminded her of Lucky. Here were brief accounts of a couple of dozen prostitutes, among them Blonde Mollie, who'd been murdered by Buckskin Frank Leslie; Gold Dollar who, in a jealous rage, had stabbed another prostitute to death one night in the Bird Cage; Crazy Horse Lil, notorious for participating in drunken brawls; Lizette the Flying Nymph, who'd come to Tombstone with a carnival and stayed to work the bordellos. Information on all of these women was sketchy at best.

She found nothing about Little Josie Blue Eyes. Had Josie been killed by her husband? Thinking about her now, Sarah felt tears well into her eyes.

After a lunch of chicken salad and homemade flour tortillas, Sarah was restless. The pool gleaming outside the glass doors was inviting.

"I'm leaving for the day," Scott's housekeeper announced when she cleared away the lunch dishes.

"There are colas or beer, or anything you might like in the kitchen. Help yourself. Mr. MacInnes probably won't be in for another couple of hours."

Rosa bounced happily away. Sarah wondered if she lived in one of the outbuildings or if she had a family in town.

She buried herself in the books again, until she grew too restless, too encumbered by memories of Lucky. There was no joy in remembering the abrupt way she'd left him. The poor kid must have wakened from his shock-and-alcohol-induced sleep and simply found her gone. He must have looked for her and wondered why she'd left him. The sadness was as strong today as it had been in the beginning.

Angry with herself for succumbing to it, Sarah closed the books and returned them carefully to the shelves. She wandered out of the library and through the quiet house, inspecting the Navajo rugs and Hopi baskets, trying to imagine what the place must have been like when Scott's great-great-grandparents had lived here.

The structure surrounded a patio. One wing was taken up by Scott's bedroom, a large, sparsely furnished space with a king-size bed and the television set he claimed never to watch. A black-and-brown-and-turquoise quilt was spread over the bed, and there was little clutter other than magazines and books. She entered the room, curious to glimpse something of the private life of this rather mysterious man. There ought to be photographs here, at least one of an attractive woman. But there were none.

Sunlight shone through the slats of the window shade, casting bands of light and shadow across the room. Following the bands of light, Sarah's eyes came to rest on a six-foot-long dresser of some dark wood. On one corner of it a glass bird sat.

Her heart stopped, then started beating again somewhere in her throat.

How could this be?

Trembling, she picked up the bird and held it. Tears rolled down her cheeks. The last time she'd seen it—the mate to her own china bird—it had been in Lucky's hand. Twenty years ago! How had Scott MacInnes gotten hold of it?

Did he know anything about the bird, whom it had belonged to? Why did he keep it here among his personal things and not on a shelf in the library with the other stuff from the past? It wasn't the sort of thing a cowboy would be drawn to.

Sarah held the bird and time went away. Her tears fell upon it, made it shine and gave it life. This was more than she had ever hoped for. If Scott would sell it to her, she'd pay almost anything....

Reluctantly she replaced it upon the dresser, then picked it up again, feeling an overwhelming desire to clutch it to her chest and never let it go. It took all her willpower to put it down again.

Still dazed, she changed into her one-piece white swimsuit in the guest bathroom in the adjacent wing, helped herself to a bath towel, and walked barefoot over the sun-warmed tiles of the spacious back patio.

The day was balmy with no breeze; a sleepy desert afternoon with the peaceful sounds of birds in the cottonwood trees. The pool shone in the sunshine. Only a few miles south, beyond the blue mountains, was Mexico.

She didn't see Scott anywhere in the corrals. Bursting with impatience to question him about the glass bird, Sarah dived into the water without testing the temperature. She swam hard, working off some of the emotional energy that was sending her crazy.

Breathing heavily, she eventually climbed out, spread her towel on a chaise longue and closed her eyes. Last night's dream about Lucky surfaced once again.

THE SPLASHING OF WATER startled her. She hadn't heard him approach. Her eyes shot open.

"Sorry if I woke you," Scott called out.

"I don't think I was asleep." She watched him swim the length of the pool and back.

He swam to the poolside and threw water at her. "In case you were, that'll keep you awake. Did it go okay today?"

"Oh, yes. Your library is impressive." She wiped the drops from her face.

"Are you coming back in?"

"I guess not. The water is wonderful, but I was in an awfully long time."

"Okay," he said agreeably. "I'll work out some kinks. I swim every day after work, summer and winter."

That had to be why he owned a heated pool. Although first impressions could be wrong, she felt he led the life of a loner, though he didn't look like a man without a social life. Women around here must keep a sharp eye on a prosperous, unmarried cowboy who looked like this guy.

That unidentifiable restlessness had returned the minute she saw Scott again. This time it was even worse; now she knew he possessed something that had once been hers, but couldn't tell him so without sounding crazy.

He swam several laps before he pulled his husky, nearly naked body out of the water. Sarah drew in her breath. Scott was almost too beautiful. While he picked up a towel, her eyes moved over him unashamedly, over his broad chest, his waist, his thighs . . .

She felt faint. A swirl of dizziness overtook her, as if the clouds in the sky were spinning in great circles.

That scar on his thigh!

Shaped like an L, the scar was exactly the shape of Lucky's wound! Numbness—disbelief—left her too weak to sit up as he approached.

How could it be anything else but the wound Josie had stitched with a needle and thread?

This scar *and* the bird? Her brain whirled. The sky-blue eyes and the familiar, mischievous smile . . . *Lord in heaven! He couldn't be anyone else!*

He sat down beside her while he dried his face and arms. "Ah! That's better! I must have left a layer of dust at the bottom of the pool. The gelding I was breaking threw me on my ass three times today."

She sat paralyzed, mesmerized by the sight of the scar on his leg, not hearing what he was saying, only taking in the way he spoke, pausing between sentences as Lucky had done.

"Lucky..." she breathed, feeling tipsy. "Lucky..."

Scott laughed. "Lucky the old rogue didn't kill me, I hope you mean. Yeah, maybe. I've been thrown twice by one horse before, but three times? Never. This was a first. Guess I'd better drag out some liniment tonight." He dried his hair vigorously. "Did you learn anything fascinating today, Sarah?"

"Yes." What if she were to blurt everything out, then find by some crazy trick of fate she was mistaken? She couldn't be, but it couldn't be true, either.

It was impossible! Before anything else was said, she wanted proof. The more she studied him, the less she doubted, but how on earth could she bring this up? Dizziness threatened to overcome her, and she thought again of last night's dream. In her subconscious she had known all along who he was!

"Well?" he asked. "What fascinating things did you learn?"

"I don't think you're going to believe me."

"If you got it out of one of my books, how could I not believe? Not that plenty of lies haven't been printed. If that's the case, I can set the record straight."

His eyes took on a silvery sheen in the approaching twilight. Her heart pounding like a drum, Sarah had to look away. It would be better to confront him with something he could see. "Scott, will you drive in to town with me? There is something I have to show you."

"Honey, I've seen everything in town."

"No you haven't. Not this. Will you?"

"Sure. Right after dinner."

"No," she insisted, hearing her voice grow stronger. "I mean now. Right now. It's very important."

He combed his fingers through his wet hair. "Hey, so is my appetite."

"We'll come back then, if you still have an appetite...."

Her request clearly didn't please him. "What could be so important that it can't wait a couple of hours? Even one? I've been looking forward to this dinner all day."

"So have I, Scott, but something has changed."

He turned. "Man, I'll say. Your voice, your eyes. You looked scared, Sarah. What the hell is wrong?"

"Not a thing is wrong." *Does he recognize anything about me? Even subconsciously? My laughter? He said my laughter reminded him of a song....*

Could it really be true that she had found Lucky again? *Could* it? Or was she dreaming?

Rising from the chaise longue, her knees would barely hold her weight. Sarah wobbled, then straightened bravely, feeling as if she'd downed too many drinks and was trying to appear sober.

"Something is wrong," he insisted, clearly concerned now.

"I'll explain in town. Can't we just get a quick shower and drive in?"

"To where?"

"My motel."

He grinned. "Okay, sure. You'll get no argument from me there."

She rolled her eyes. "Be as flip as you like, Mr. MacInnes. It won't last when you see what I want to show you."

He rose, still rubbing his hair with a towel. "You know, pretty lady, we're alone out here. There is all the privacy in the world here. We don't have to go in to a motel."

"Will you stop? I can't tell whether you're misjudging or teasing, but it had better be the latter!" She stood in front of him, feeling the breeze blowing through her hair, and gazing deeply into his blue eyes. *My God, they're Lucky's eyes!*

Scott blinked. The sensations brought on by this woman's inviting eyes, by the golden reflections of the sunset in her hair, were almost more than he could bear. Why was she looking at him like that? The urge to touch her was almost overpowering, but he fought it down. It was hard enough just to avoid staring at her in that white swimsuit, it revealed so much of her shapely body. If he weren't careful, he would run with her signals and make a fool of himself.

What the devil bothered him so about her? Her beauty? What else could it be?

He cursed himself. It had been too long since he had been with a woman. He cursed his life. He cursed the currents in his body that raced like electricity in his blood whenever he so much as glanced at her. Yet whatever it was lay deeper. It bothered him.

Sarah was acting as if she was in a hurry. She was already inside the house and had disappeared into the guest wing. He heard the shower running. In his own suite, Scott showered quickly, pulled on jeans, a gray, Western-cut shirt and boots, and was in the kitchen wolfing down one of Rosa's tamales by the time his guest found him.

"Have a tamale," he offered.

"I couldn't possibly eat. I'm too excited."

"Well, I'm starved. I've been thinking about these tamales all day."

"Can't you hurry?"

"Eat faster? I'm choking already." He pushed the plate toward her. "Here. Wouldn't hurt to build up your energy. It might be a while before we get a chance to finish them."

"Oh, Scott! Who cares about food?" She was flying around the kitchen like a child waiting to go to a circus. What the devil had gotten into her? But whatever it was, he liked it.

"Scott, life is just so . . . just so incredible. It's just a mystery. An unfathomable mystery. I can't believe I found my way out here . . . to you . . . I just can't!"

"Neither can I," he said, returning the dish to the refrigerator. Maybe she had helped herself to a drink in his bar, but she hadn't seemed intoxicated at the pool. Now she was acting high as a kite. What was he in for when they got to town?

He insisted on driving. During the twenty-mile ride, she said very little, but he could feel her eyes on him every moment. He tried to prepare himself for anything.

The motel was on the outskirts of Tombstone, with a view of the vast valley and the town. "Ah," he said suddenly. "Fireworks!"

"You know?"

"About the fireworks? Sure. I hate to spoil your surprise, but the town often has fireworks displays. But you're right—this is a great place to watch them."

Sarah's heart thumped in her chest. They were almost there. "Wrong. I didn't know about the fireworks. Is it a special occasion?"

He shrugged. "I don't know. I thought you did."

"Oh, it is! You'd better believe it. No one knows it but me, and soon you."

She was stiffening with fear. Was she wrong about this whole crazy thing? Had her imagination run amok? But if it was true . . . if he was Lucky, it wouldn't be the same. He had been just a kid then. He was a man now, with a man's soul and cynicism. Even if it was somehow true, would he believe it? Would he still care? There was a darkness about Scott MacInnes. Even if he had been Lucky, he was not that child now.

Worst of all, what if he didn't remember? Or what if the scar was only a coincidence? The eyes, though...his eyes... She was trembling hard by the time they reached the door of her room. The key shook in her hand, and he had to take over and put it into the lock.

"My curiosity has reached wild heights," he said, switching on the light. He looked at her in the sudden brightness. "Sarah, are you okay? You're so pale. Are you taking drugs?"

She shook her head. "Of course not." Their eyes met. "Okay, we're here. The thing I want to show you is here. I don't have to tell you what it is. You'll see it if you look."

"Do I get a hint? Is it bigger than a—?"

He stopped abruptly. In the stark motel room there wasn't much of interest to see, only a few of Sarah's belongings on the dresser. A glass bird sat alone on the bed table. For a moment, it shimmered and seemed to come alive in the lamplight.

Sarah watched him carefully. He blinked and blinked again, rushed to the dresser and picked up the bird. Turning it over and over in his hand, he asked in a strange, husky voice, "Where did you get this?"

"Where did you get yours? I saw it when I was giving myself a tour of your house today."

His eyes had gone almost blank; he spoke in a monotone. "I've had it a long time."

"Since you were eleven?"

He stared at her, visibly too shocked to speak. Aware that he was studying her face, she knew his mind was whirling too fast for him to find his voice. Her eyes filled with tears while heartbeats thundered in her ears. As she gazed at him, her lips formed his name.

"Lucky?"

He stood like a statue, frozen.

Tears streamed down her cheeks. "I'm Sally."

His eyes clouded. The hand holding the bird began to tremble. "How—?" Blinking moisture from his eyes, Scott slowly, silently opened his arms.

She rushed to him. He grasped her as if to save her from a fatal fall and held her tightly against his chest; she could barely breathe. His silence filled a hundred years.

"It's true, then!" she said abruptly. "It's true! You are Lucky. I saw the scar on your thigh. I kept telling myself it couldn't be, and I had to see your reaction to the bird to prove to myself . . ."

His voice sounded like an echo. "You are Sally. I can see it now. Your face hasn't changed that much. No wonder you were driving me crazy without my knowing why! You found me again and I didn't know you."

He held her as if he never intended to release her, never intended to let her get away again. His heart beat hard against hers.

"I didn't recognize you, either. But how could we? We wouldn't have thought in a million years that we would ever see each other again."

"This is impossible," he muttered.

"No, *this* is possible. Our first meeting . . . that was impossible."

Scott finally drew away, sat down on the edge of the bed and held his head in his hands. "I'm sorry.... I suddenly don't feel good...."

"You're not going to faint, are you?"

"Men don't faint."

"Oh, I see. But they do lose consciousness occasionally from shock."

"Nah. I just have to...absorb this for a minute. Everything started to go a little dark there, and I was afraid I was being pulled back in time again. A black spiral. It was starting."

She plopped onto the bed beside him. "Yes, there was a spiral! I experienced it, too. You had it *now?*"

He nodded, plainly confused. "You too? Are you saying you didn't live in Tombstone then? You haven't come to me from the past?"

"No! No. I somehow spiraled back there on my eleventh birthday, the day I found the glass bird in my grandmother's attic. When I was looking at it, I grew dizzy, everything went black, and the next thing I knew I was in the Bird Cage Theater with Josie. And then with you."

He rubbed his eyes. "All these years I thought...I assumed you had lived and died a long time ago."

"I assumed the same about you. But I thought of you every single day of my life."

He looked at her. She saw his hands were still trembling. "Your name is Sarah?"

All the way here in his car, she had wondered what he'd say first. She hadn't thought about her name, but about his. "Sally is a nickname for Sarah. And you? You aren't Lucky anymore?"

"That started when I was eight years old and won three kids' rodeo trophies in one day. The announcer gave me the name and it stuck. Some people around town still call me Lucky." He shook his head, as if trying to shake out cobwebs. "How did you find me?"

"I don't know. I always wanted to come to Tombstone to see what it looks like now. Most of my life I convinced myself it had all been a dream and there was no reason to come. But I read everything I could find about Tombstone, nevertheless, and recently I've been compelled to write about it. Lately I've wanted to write about the people I met there. Not you, though. I thought it would be too painful writing about you. Oh, I missed you so! You can't imagine how I missed you!"

"I can imagine," he said softly. "I can imagine very well."

She knelt beside him, resting her weight on his knees. "Scott, what's the last thing you remember?"

"Falling asleep with my leg hurting like hell and the whiskey making me sick." He paused, frowning. "No, the last thing I remember is you handing me that glass bird and saying they were a pair. One was yours and one was mine and they would always be together. The next thing I knew, I was in the hayloft of the barn and my leg was killing me. I had such a death grip on that glass sparrow, it's a wonder I didn't break it."

"The last thing," she whispered, "was the two birds touching each other. That's when I felt myself being pulled back to my own time. I was terrified that you would think I left you."

He smiled softly and caressed her hair. "So was I. For twenty years I've worried about what happened to you."

Wiping her tears, Sarah tried to imagine what it had been like for him. "How did you explain it? To your family, I mean? Was it awful trying to explain?"

"It was a nightmare. I was gone more than three days, and then I showed up with my leg stitched, muttering about a girl at the Bird Cage sewing the wound with a needle and thread. It got all over the county that I had stitched up my own leg, because there was never any other logical explanation. The doctor confirmed it was a knife wound. My family thought I'd run off into the hills to play rustler and fell on my own knife."

"Did you ever tell them the truth?"

"I tried at first. Nobody listened to the truth."

She smiled. "Yes, I know. I tried the truth, too, but not for long."

Sarah wanted to know everything, wanted all the mystery of the past solved in five minutes. "Where were you when you were pulled over the time barrier? What were you doing?"

"I was in the hayloft, throwing down hay for the horses. A sparrow flew in, and I was watching it fly around the rafters of the barn. There was only one high window and the light was strange...the hay dust made it all sparkly. I remember thinking it looked like magic. And the next thing, the spiral was in my head. I suddenly found myself in the small meadow near the barn, but everything was different . . . the house, the buildings, the people, and nobody knew me and I didn't know them."

She stroked the scar on his thigh. "How did you get into Tombstone?"

"I hitched a ride on a wagon. People at the ranch were talking about the shoot-out in town when the Earps and Doc Holliday killed Tom and Frank McLaury and Billy Clanton. The Earps' murder trial had been over for several weeks, but the furor was still going on. Some people insisted the Earps were cold-blooded killers. Others thought they were doing a lawman's job. I knew all about the gunfight because my mother taught me so much of the history. In fact, I used to pretend I was Wyatt, outdrawing the McLaurys. Then here I was, back in time. I had no idea how it happened, but I was excited as hell. I wanted to see the heroes of the OK Corral fight in person."

"So you had already been there, exploring, when I met you."

"Yeah. I had been all over. The town looked a lot the same." He continued to stroke her hair. "Where did you come from, Sarah? California, like you said?"

"Los Angeles. I was in my grandmother's attic, looking at a trunk full of old clothes. I remember coming down afterward, thinking it was the same day as when I went up there, but people and cops were all over the house and all the neighbors were looking for me. It seems I'd been missing for twenty-four hours. I hid the bird in my pocket and then later in my room. No one ever saw it, because I didn't want my grandmother to take it away from me. It's been my secret ever since. I knew it was magical." Her voice quivered. "And I knew you had the other one . . . and I thought you were still there . . . back in time."

"All the while I was here," he said softly. "Being haunted by memories of you."

Sarah sniffed, trying to hold back another flood of tears. "I don't know what this all means. Maybe it means we are supposed to be together."

Scott squeezed her hand. "It has to mean that. Who decided it though, Sarah?"

She tried to smile. "Who decided? You're asking me who or what controls fate? If I knew that I'd be God."

"Then I suppose it's useless to try to reason it out. We've lost so many years when we could have been together. I looked for you in every girl I ever met. Tried to talk myself out of my obsession, but always, time and time again, I would leave them because they weren't you."

"I've done the same damn thing! I thought I would be alone forever, cursed with—" Suddenly she became self-conscious. This wasn't Lucky the boy she was talking to. This was a big, brutally handsome man who, only yesterday, had been a stranger.

And he had that darkness. Sarah had felt it last night and again today. Underneath the surface was a complex human being and something mysterious, something dark. She had known a tough little kid for a day and a half. This man she did not know.

But she knew he still had that tough edge.

And she knew now he had not forgotten her. Was that good or bad? How far did the connection go? What if, as adults with very different life-styles, they were not compatible and there was no way to . . . to . . . ?

"What's the matter?" Scott asked, taking her hands and pulling her onto the bed beside him.

"It's scary."

"Are you afraid of me?"

"I don't know, Scott. I'm afraid of this whole weird situation."

"You weren't afraid of me, then."

"No."

"I would still protect you with my life."

"Would you?" She gazed at him. "Why?"

"Why?" He leaned over and brushed his lips gently across her cheek. "You know why. Because I love you."

6

SARAH'S KNEES WENT WEAK. She had heard the echo of the words "I love you" over and over again during the past twenty years. And had said so easily then, and with such conviction, "I love you, too."

"You still love me," Scott whispered, as if he had read her mind. "Otherwise you wouldn't have found me."

It was true. She had loved Lucky so completely all her life that there had never been room for anyone else. What was she so afraid of, all of a sudden? Just the incredibility of it all? The fact that there was no reality under her feet?

"I'm the same person," he said, reading her mind again.

She smiled, remembering sleeping next to him in the tiny, old-fashioned hotel room. "Are you? Are you still that kid who dreams about meeting Wyatt Earp?"

"I've always wanted to go back."

"To meet the Earps or to find me?"

"To find you, make no mistake about that. I wanted to find you again and stay with you forever and keep you safe. I wanted to live in your time. I was always convinced I belonged back there. Maybe we both did."

She couldn't help staring at his eyes. All the memories of them together were mirrored there. "The excite-

ment electrified you so much you wanted to be part of
it. You had to have that gun, remember?"

"And you," he teased, "didn't want to wear a dress
and black stockings, and I didn't blame you. Thinking
back now, I might have wondered about your wearing
jeans and sandals, but I was no expert on what kids of
that day wore, and an eleven-year-old doesn't think
much about what girls are wearing. I wasn't seeing you
the way the others did, and in all these years since it just
never dawned on me that you were as much a stranger
to that century as I was."

Sarah grinned. "*I* was wild about Josie's satin gowns.
What do you think happened to her?"

"I've often wondered." Scott touched her cheek with
the backs of his fingers. "You're even more beautiful
than you were then," he said huskily. "I've often tried
to picture how you looked as a woman, but I didn't
picture you as lovely as you are, your hair soft as silk.
Before I left Nellie Cashman's hotel I touched your hair
in the morning when you were asleep. I lay beside you
and watched you sleep and touched your hair, then I
kissed your cheek and you smiled."

She flushed. His touch now was so sensuous; how
could she ever have slept through such an invasion of
the depths of her heart? Even at eleven, he had understood physical attraction very well.

Scott's lips moved across her cheek and forehead,
and finally her lips. Slowly, gently, he was taking possession of her, as he had done before.

Her blood turned to syrup, her heart grew wings. When he kissed her, she soared to heights she had never seen, somewhere above and beyond the mountains, above and beyond the earth...where she could get hopelessly lost if she tried to stay....

"I've waited so long for you," he whispered.

Tiny prickles of fear began to shoot through her. Something felt wrong. "Scott, I don't...*I don't know you....*"

"You've always known me," he contradicted.

"I knew a boy, but you're a man I met only a few hours ago. I don't know who you are."

"Maybe," he offered, "those little glass sparrows are still too far apart, are still looking for each other. Let's go get mine and see if their magic will make you love me the way you loved me then."

"Get the birds together again? Aren't you a little afraid to do that, after experiencing the spiral today?"

His thick, dark eyebrows rose. "Why? You don't think it could happen again?"

"I have no idea. I don't know why it happened the first time." The excitement blazing in Scott's eyes frightened Sarah.

"Maybe it could happen again!" he exclaimed. "Maybe we could go back!"

"What?"

"To 1882! If the birds touch each other again, maybe the magic could take us back!"

"Why in heaven's name would you want to?" she asked, but already knew the answer. Even as she spoke the words, the crazy idea was gripping her with a sense of wild excitement.

"I've always wanted to go back! I told you, I think I was supposed to live then."

"Well, I wasn't. I happen to like the twentieth century." *Imagine the research, though. Think what I could do with my script if I could experience that life firsthand again.*

"I wonder if there's a chance?" He seemed not to have heard her mild protest. "I tried it a hundred times, even went to a hypnotist. Maybe those sparrows are as magical as you say. Do you really think they are what transported us across time?"

Sarah couldn't decide whether she wanted to hear this or not. "Why do you call them sparrows?"

He shrugged. "They look like sparrows to me. I was looking at a sparrow in the hayloft that day."

"And I was looking at the figurine I'd just found in my grandmother's trunk. And a bird was singing in the attic window."

Scott jumped to his feet and pulled her up with him. "Let's go get my sparrow! Let's see if the pair are the trigger to going back!" His eyes were aglow. "Think of it, Sally...Sarah...my love...think of us finding our love again there, where we first found it!"

Fear of the unknown mysteries of time and space tempered the wild rush of adventure. Her heart was beating too fast. "Wait a minute! We have to talk about this!"

"We'll talk. We have plenty of time to talk in the car." Excitedly he grabbed the figurine from the bed table.

"Be careful, you'll break it," Sarah warned. "If you're that rough with mine, how have you kept from breaking yours all these years?"

"Like you, I hid it and it stayed hidden all the time I was growing up. Once in a while I would take it out and look at it. No one ever knew. How would I have explained having a sissy bird figurine in my room?"

Sarah picked up her handbag and took the bird as he hurried her out the door. The evening cool was descending. It might have been a good idea to change from her miniskirt into a pair of jeans, but they were already outside when she thought of it. No matter, it was warm in the car.

Scott stopped in the twilight shadows before they got in, took her into his arms and gazed at her as if gazing at a dazzling sunrise. "You've come back to me," he whispered. "I don't know how, or what forces are guiding us. But you've come back to me. . . ." His eyes closed. "You've come back to me. . . ."

Emotion almost choked her. "Something *has* guided me to you again."

"Something strange and wonderful." He hugged her tighter. "Beyond wonderful!"

He opened the car door for her, then got into the driver's seat. "We met on the stage of the Bird Cage Theater, and we parted in the same place. I think the birds and the Bird Cage have something to do with each other. If we want to give this experiment every chance, we ought to try it there where it happened before."

"You might be right," she agreed, allowing Scott's excitement to override her concerns for a moment. The mystery and intrigue of going back! Being there with Lucky—with Scott—again! Her dream come true.

"There's something else," she went on. "Today's my birthday. It happened before on my birthday."

"Today? How old?"

"Thirty-one."

"I'll be damned! I turned thirty-one the day before yesterday. It happened to me on my eleventh birthday, too. You never mentioned it was your birthday! You didn't then . . . or now."

"We were born within hours of each other! Day before yesterday—your birthday—I had a dream about us in Tombstone. I mean a dream about Lucky and Sally. That day I took my glass bird out of hiding and packed it in my suitcase to bring it with me . . . to bring it home."

"What do you mean, bring it home?"

"You couldn't have known Josie owned the second bird, the one I have now. She got it from an old Gypsy who promised if she ever found its mate, she would find her true and forever love. Josie said all she found was me, standing in the theater, holding the mate to hers. So she gave it to me and told me I might have better luck, that maybe I would find my true and forever love. A few minutes later you appeared."

Scott rubbed his neck as though it was stiff. "I thought you brought the birds with you when you ran away from home."

"I've no idea how my grandmother came to have the bird, and by the time I was old enough to realize it was important to ask, she had died. I don't know if the birds are magical or not." Wondering, worrying, they finished the ride in silence. Scott made straight for his bedroom and brought out the figurine, which looked very small and delicate in his hand.

Sarah gazed at it, remembering her dream about his hands.

"Are you shivering?" he asked.

"The night is getting cold." She didn't know whether the cold was making her shiver, or whether it was the uncanny surprises of the past few hours. "Can I borrow a jacket?"

"There in the coat closet," he said. "Take your pick."

She chose a Western-cut leather jacket with fringes on the back and sleeves; she'd always wanted to wear a jacket like that. It was too big, and it hung loosely on her nearly to the bottom of her short skirt, but it made her somehow less vulnerable to be wrapped in something Scott had worn. And worn often, from the look of it.

"Ready?" he asked.

She held out her hand and he carefully laid the bird in her palm. This was the one she'd found in the attic, the one she was holding when she found herself in the theater. Now to be holding it again . . .

"Are you all right?" he asked. "You look as dazed as I feel."

She held tightly to the past and nodded.

"Hang on, I'll be right back." Scott disappeared for a short time into his room and returned carrying a jacket over his arm.

Outside, about to open the door for her, he stopped, took her into his arms and kissed her. "Happy birthday, Sarah. I'm going to find you a birthday present."

His kiss drained what little energy she had left. If he hadn't been holding her, her knees might have buckled. "A birthday present isn't necessary. . . ."

"Of course it is. This day calls for celebrations like we've never had before." He kissed her again, longer, deeper than before. "How can life change so drastically in only an hour? I can't believe I have you back."

"Other boys might have forgotten," she said, gently touching his handsome face.

"Other boys have never met you."

He kissed her again, yielding to passion. Around them the winter twilight darkened the open, quiet spaces that were Scott's private world. The peaceful sounds of a horse's whinny and of the dogs brushing through the grass left Sarah feeling as though nothing here was quite real . . . not the place, nor the hour, not even Scott.

"Will it be open?" she asked listlessly.

"What?" His breath was warm on her ear.

"The Bird Cage Theater. Can we get in?"

He drew away and looked at his watch. "Yeah, if we don't waste any time, it will still be open. This is a big month for tourists." He opened the car door for her.

They rode in silence for a while, his glass bird in her hand, hers still tucked in the glove compartment. As they neared town, she asked nervously, "Scott?"

"Yeah?"

"Are we really going to try this?"

"Why not? It probably won't work. Magic doesn't work for adults like it does for kids. So we'll experiment for old times' sake. Afterward we'll have dinner in town. You must be hungry."

"I hadn't thought about it."

"My stomach is growling. We'll have dinner in town after we've shown the sparrows the Bird Cage again."

THERE WERE ONLY four tourists in the theater, two couples, one young, one old. Since their first visit a partition had been erected between the bar and the theater proper so that the stage could no longer be seen from the front door. Scott, who knew the man in charge, bought two tickets, and they proceeded through a small doorway into the heart of the musty old opera house, as Sarah had done the day before. Overhead, manikins looked down at them from the cages; the blue and gold wallpaper had faded and the maroon velvet curtains grown dusty. Under the balconies was a collection of circus posters that looked a century old, but they had not been there in the early part of 1882.

Over the stage the painted floral design was faded, but still clearly visible.

"It's eerie how this building is so well preserved," Sarah said. "Gives me a funny feeling."

Scott nodded. "The place is haunted. Through the years I've seldom come in here because of the ghosts—and because it bothered me too much to think of her . . . of you." Circling her waist with one arm, he led her past the grand piano, up the steps and onto the stage. Sarah felt giddy; she was here again with Lucky! Yet the man whose arm encircled her wasn't a mischievous kid. This was a six-foot-tall cowboy she barely knew.

"I remember it vividly," he said. "You standing up here all alone and looking lost. I pulled back the curtain and thought I was looking at an angel."

"I was standing just here." She moved downstage, estimating the spot. "And the last day, Josie and the other woman, Pearl, moved you and the cot over to this side. Wasn't it about here?"

"You'd know that better than I would. I wasn't feeling too alert at the time." He looked about. "This is a good time to try it, Sarah, when nobody else is on the stage. Let's find out if our glass-feathered friends are really magic."

A chilly sensation—was it fear?—moved through her. *Lord in heaven, what if this works?* What if she really did go back in time with this man she was just a little afraid of? Knowing the boy he once was . . . loving the boy he once was . . . wasn't the same as loving a stranger. She knew so little about him.

No, it wouldn't work. Neither of them really believed it would, but somehow they had to try for the sake of their memories. Sooner or later they would try, so it might as well be sooner. Still unsure, Sarah dug into the pockets of Scott's fringed jacket and took out the birds.

These are just pieces of glass. Her fear gave way to a sense of intrigue. To the recognition of the miracle they both had experienced long ago. In a very private and secret way they were bonding again.

Sarah realized she wanted this to work more than she feared returning to the past. Her excitement was building. No question about it, her love for Lucky was proving to be far, far stronger than her fear of Scott.

"Hold me," she said. "In the unlikely event that we are able to do this, I don't want us to get separated again."

"God forbid," Scott breathed and drew her close. "I've just found you. I have no intention of losing you again. Wherever time takes us, we're going together."

He took one sparrow from her, they clasped hands over the little figurines and let their wings touch.

The spirals circled down, too fast for either of them to speak. Everything went black, and in a time frame they could neither count nor comprehend the blackness turned into light.

Blinding light. Stage light. They heard boisterous laughter, shouts and howls. Loud piano music.

The curtain was open. Mustached men were clapping and yelling at them. Scott had a hard grip on her arm.

"It worked! We've done it!" he said over the din.

"Oh, my God!" She gazed down, taking in the drunken smiles, the wild eyes and the whiskey glasses waving in the air. Men were yelling at them . . . no, at *her!* One look at her miniskirt and red cotton turtleneck sweater under the fringed jacket, and they seemed to have assumed she was part of the entertainment.

"They think you're going to perform," Scott said, his voice strange. Was he trying to conceal the shock of defying linear time once again? "Do something, Sarah. Dance."

"Me? You dance!"

The demands were growing louder. Miners just off their shift were waving their arms and shouting. The shouting was good-natured, but nevertheless, these men could be frightening if they were riled. They ignored the cowboy on stage: all eyes were on Sarah. Even dance-hall girls didn't expose their bare legs as Sarah's were in the mini. The rowdy audience was getting very excited.

She was horrified. "Let's get out of here!" Desperate, she looked for an exit.

Scott moved closer, which didn't please the theater's clientele. "It'll cause a riot if you walk off this stage. Those guys mean business. Most of them have been underground for the past eight hours and they paid hard-earned money for the show. They think that includes your performance."

"Great! Just great! What do I do? I can't possibly dance to this stupid music!"

"Sing, then."

"Sing? To *this?*"

"I think you'd better sing," he said helplessly.

Sarah looked down; just below the stage a man was pounding away at the giant piano. She moved to the edge. Even this slight movement, which made the jacket's fringe weave with her body, started the audience howling. She thought of screaming rock fans.

The piano player was a professional. The moment he saw she wanted his attention, he stopped and stood up to talk to her. "What'll it be?" he asked, chewing on a crudely rolled cigarette.

"I don't think you'd know any songs that I know...."

"Go ahead and begin, Lassie. Don't worry. I'll fill in."

She looked helplessly at Scott. The truth was, Sarah loved to sing. She'd been a soloist in high school glee club. But this . . .

Trembling, she gestured to show she was ready to begin, and the opera house grew deathly still. Even at the far end, where men were gathered around the bar, the noise ceased. Taking a step forward, Sarah opened her mouth. "How—" Her voice cracked. She paused and started again, gathering courage. Quietly at first, her voice grew stronger as she sang the first song that popped into her head—"How Much Is That Doggie in the Window?"

Every eye was fixed on her. Though the setting was bizarre, Sarah began to enjoy the devoted attention. When she finished the song the applause was wild. Scott gave her a thumbs-up from the far side of the stage.

The pianist made a victory sign and waited for his next cue. Sarah frantically sorted through her repertoire of Elvis songs. "Hound Dog." No, two dog songs in a row wouldn't be a great choice. Her records had been played so often, she'd memorized the words to every song.

She was having fun. Swinging her arms and hips, she hit a strong note and began "Heartbreak Hotel."

As she moved, the fringes of Scott's jacket swayed to and fro. The song hushed the crowd.

By the time she'd finished, Sarah was feeling the heat of the gas spotlights, so she removed the jacket and threw it to the back of the stage where Scott stood watching her entranced.

The audience was so wild by this time that men were standing and waving their hats in the air. Sarah smiled and took a deep bow, arms outstretched. She was worried about making her exit. The best thing would be to just get off quickly, so she beat a hasty retreat to the back of the stage. Three Oriental dancing girls covered with feathers were waiting to go on. One of them smiled at her, then they ran on to meet the cheers of the audience.

Scott clasped his arms around her. "You pulled it off! What a woman!"

"Some choice I had," Sarah said, elated with her success. "Since I'm a lousy dancer, it was either sing or strip."

The look he gave her was sober. "Don't even joke like that. Having to *sing* in a bordello is bad enough."

The music was gay and tinny, the voices rowdy. Sarah put the jacket on again and gave Scott's arm an affectionate squeeze. "I rather love this bordello! The magic is real. We're actually back in the place where we met!"

"Yeah." He grinned. "We've done it!" As he took her hand, she recognized the sparkle in his eyes, the same excitement that had lighted Lucky's eyes. Excitement at being in a frontier boomtown.

"Let's go," he said.

"Go where? I want to look for Josie."

He led Sarah to the top of the back stairs. They heard gruff voices and smelled cigar smoke from a card game going on below. "And say what to her?" Scott asked. "If you find Josie, she won't recognize you. In fact, the first thing we need to do is find out what the date is. Hell, we don't know for sure what *year* this is."

The props in the stage area looked the same as those Sarah remembered. Now she smelled canvas and cheap perfume, where only moments before the place had been empty, reeking of dust and mildew. While the dancing girls performed, there were no other people behind these back curtains; soon, though, someone was going to show up and ask them who the devil they were and why she'd been up there performing. There would be explaining to do.

Sarah looked down at herself. "How could I have been stupid enough to wear a miniskirt?"

"Don't be so hard on yourself. It was a spur-of-the-moment plan and we didn't expect it to work."

"I've got to get a dress, though. I can't wear this on the street."

"You definitely can't. Okay. Wait here while I find a shop open and buy you a dress."

"With what? Your Visa card, maybe?"

He laughed. "Haven't you noticed I'm wearing a sterling silver belt buckle?"

She had noticed it, of course; who could not? The thing was as big as her fist. "You'd buy a dress for me before you'd purchase a gun?"

"I have a gun. I brought two."

"What?"

"Inside my jacket. That's what I went back for...just in case this long shot of an experiment worked."

Guns. A chill shot through her body. And Scott considered himself a crack shot. Oh, God!

He was standing on the top step, ready to start down. Exactly like long ago. They were replaying the scene, except that it was night now and the theater was noisy. She tugged at his sleeve. "Just what are you planning to do with those guns?"

"Since we couldn't bring money, I figured modern guns would be in demand. Besides," he said softly, "I know what it's like here. I have to protect my lady."

Fear tugged at her heart. "Like before?"

His eyes hardened. "No, not like before. This time no cheating bully with a big mouth is going to get the better of me."

She clung to him. "You're scaring me."

He smiled. "This is a wide-open town, honey, but you don't have anything to be afraid of as long as I'm here."

"Oh, don't I? You could get yourself killed."

He took her hand from his arm and kissed her fingers lightly. "Danger is part of living here. Don't turn chicken on me, Sally. Just enjoy this while you can . . . while we can." He turned. "Now I'm off to buy you a fine dress."

"You don't know my size."

He held out his hands, curving his fingers. "You're only this big. Trust me. If anyone asks what you're doing here—"

"I'll make up something. Just don't take all night and don't get anything purple. I look awful in purple."

She watched him disappear down the steps. They were reliving the past. Would he sleep beside her tonight, as he had done then? The thought brought shivers and a sense of anticipation.

She remembered his guns and shivered again. At least half the drunken men out there were toting guns. People got shot here for the most trivial reasons.

It dawned on Sarah that this wasn't a game. He'd been badly hurt the last time. This time . . .

What did he mean by saying he had to protect his lady? Protect her from what?

7

SARAH WAS INDIGNANT. She wasn't a kid now, someone who needed protecting. At least she wouldn't need
protecting as soon as she changed into something more
suitable.

She looked at the two glass birds in her hands—their
tickets for the trip across the time barrier. It was too
risky to carry them around; she had to hide them. Why
not here backstage, as she had done before? Along the
unfinished walls were props, costumes, and a million
crannies where no one would ever find them.

Ducking behind two inner curtains, she found a niche
against the wall studs behind some boxes, almost where
she had hidden them before. "Keep safe, my darlings,"
she whispered, stroking each figurine lovingly. "You're
our only way home." She placed them in her leather
handbag and hid it well, behind a dusty box.

The feathered dancers left the stage and an acrobatic
act went on. No one noticed her behind the inner curtain. Sarah made her way along the sidewall, where she
could peer through the curtains into the theater without being seen. She was hoping for a glimpse of Josie.
The women in the crowd were easy to spot by their
bright colored dresses—splashes of scarlet, emerald
green and turquoise in a brown and khaki sea.

One of the scarlet splashes was the dress Josie had been wearing the last time Sarah had seen her. Her white-blond curls attracted even more attention than the dress. Josie was talking animatedly with a red-bearded man. They were on the edge of the crowd, along the theater side, where gambling tables were set up. Sarah didn't like what she saw. The man's hand was grasping Josie's arm tightly, and Josie was trying to pull away. She looked frightened.

Whatever the man said made Josie shake her head vehemently. Another man stood up and urged the red-bearded man to his table. As he retreated he raised a fist threateningly. Josie backed away, too, rubbing her injured arm. The two men sat down at the table, heads together, drinking and talking.

That must be her husband, Sarah thought. But Josie looked so young. Years younger than Sarah was now. She ached to run down, embrace her friend and find out what was going on, but knew she couldn't. Josie would have no idea who she was, and Sarah couldn't tell her.

"So here you are!" boomed a masculine voice behind her. "And without the famous blue bonnet!"

Sarah jumped and whirled around. The owner of the voice was dressed in black pants and coat over a silk shirt, and was smiling. His eyes traveled boldly the length of her body and back to her face.

"Two days late getting here. More trouble with those trains from 'Frisco? Why didn't you tell me you had arrived?"

She glanced around to see if anyone else was near, but they were alone. Whom did he believe she was?

"I'm not who you think—" she began hesitantly, trying to figure out how to explain what she was doing here.

"You're my singer from 'Frisco, of course! And a fine one, thank God. Great legs! I'm Billy Hutchinson, naturally. We gave you good press here for last weekend. I was ready to cancel your contract when you didn't get here, but . . ." He smiled broadly and took a cigar from his coat pocket. "After hearing you sing, it was worth the wait. The crowd went wild out there. And what a brilliant theatrical move, coming on unannounced like that! I love it! You had them screaming for more." He put a lighted match to the cigar and puffed hard. "I'm prepared to offer you a long-term contract, Miss Bluebonnet. You did indicate you had reason to want to leave 'Frisco for an extended time." His grin hinted at some private joke.

"I'm not Bluebonnet," Sarah said.

The owner of the Bird Cage yanked the cigar from his mouth. "She sent someone else in her place?"

"Well, no, I . . ."

His laugh was like a moose call. "Well, the truth is, Miss, I don't care who you are. I'm offering you my best contract. Six weeks to start, twelve shows a week, ninety dollars a week with one day free. Pick your free day. We're open seven days a week, twenty-four hours a day."

Stunned, Sarah merely stared at him.

He puffed on the cigar again, then smiled. "Okay, wear that costume and I'll make it a hundred."

Her mind whirled. This was a way of making a living—not an easy matter for a woman on the frontier. The incredible offer was a godsend. "I only sing," she said. "Nothing else. I don't socialize with the customers."

"You entertain only on stage. Right. Understood."

"Then we've got a deal." She smiled and extended her hand.

His handshake was so heavy, he shook her whole body. "Now, what's your billing?"

"What?"

"Your stage name."

She glanced around, trying to think fast. To her left were the narrow stairs leading to the catwalks behind the "bird cages." For some reason, her glass birds liked this crazy place. "Sparrow," she said.

"Sparrow? Sparrow what?"

She waved cigar smoke from her face. "Just . . . Sparrow."

"Beautiful! Sparrow, San Francisco Warbler." Hutchinson seemed very pleased with himself.

"There is just one thing, Mr. Hutchinson. My luggage was lost en route. I'll need an advance to buy a costume."

"What's wrong with the costume you're wearing?"

"It doesn't sparkle."

"Ahh! Right. Fine. Sparkle all you can, my little Sparrow." He reached into his pocket and handed her several bills—a hundred dollars' worth. "Now for this, how about another song?"

"Now? But I just got here and—"

"One more song. The Flying Ryans are about to come off. I'll announce you. Just one song, so I can begin the big promotion."

He obviously wouldn't take no for an answer. *I might as well get used to doing this,* she thought. In fact she was thrilled to have got the job. As a child she'd stood in front of her mirror and pretended she was singing to an audience, like the singers in the movies. She was proud of her clear voice and good range. This was going to be more fun than she'd ever had in her twentieth-century life.

What was more, the contract put her right into the Bird Cage, where she wanted to be. Where Josie was. Where she could learn more than any outsider ever would.

Still excited, she listened to the elaborate introduction. *Warbling Sparrow.* Good Lord! The clapping was so enthusiastic, they wouldn't even let her new boss finish his spiel. She took her cue and bounded onto the stage, her jacket fringes flapping wildly.

By the time the curtain came down and she had taken her last bow, Sarah felt like a pro. Her audience had made her feel that way. Mr. Hutchinson was right; they loved her and her crazy songs! Thank heavens for Elvis; she wondered how the crowd would like the Beach Boys.

GET 4 BOOKS

FREE

Return this card, and we'll send you 4 brand-new Harlequin Temptation® novels, absolutely *FREE!* We'll even pay the postage both ways!

We're making you this offer to introduce you to the benefits of the Harlequin Reader Service®: free home delivery of brand-new romance novels, before they're available in stores, **AND** at a saving of 30¢ apiece compared to the cover price!

Accepting these 4 free books places you under no obligation to continue. You may cancel at any time, even just after receiving your free shipment. If you do not cancel, every month we'll send 4 more Harlequin Temptation novels and bill you just $2.69* apiece—that's all!

Yes! Please send me my 4 free Harlequin Temptation novels, as explained above.

Name

Address   Apt.

City   State   Zip

142 CIH AGNU (U-H-T-11/92)

*Terms and prices subject to change without notice. Sales tax applicable in NY. Offer limited to one per household and not valid to current Harlequin Temptation subscribers. All orders subject to approval. © 1990 Harlequin Enterprises Limited.

Printed in Canada

Get 4 Books FREE

SEE BACK OF CARD FOR DETAILS

She saw Scott standing at the back of the stage with a garment of green velvet draped over his arms; he was scowling. "What was that all about?"

She rushed to him. "This gown! It looks gorgeous! Oh, let me see!"

"Why were you singing again?"

She reached for the dress. "It's my job. The owner offered me a hundred dollars a week to sing here."

Scott looked as if he'd been struck in the face. "You agreed?"

"Of course! For money like that? I've always wanted somebody to listen to me sing." She held up the dress and gasped. It was a two-piece suit with pearl buttons on the fitted jacket, and was trimmed with pearl-colored linen lace. A narrow, ankle-length skirt. The green velvet was so dark that it looked black in shadow and shone silver in direct light. "It's so chic, Scott! And so beautifully made! Oh, but it must have been horribly expensive . . . on your limited funds."

"I promised you a birthday present. Happy birthday, Sarah." He bent and kissed her cheek. She couldn't hug him back because the gown filled her arms. "Now," he said. "Slip it on and let's get out of here. You don't fit in this place."

She eyed him curiously. "You said much the same thing the last time." Slipping off her miniskirt, she stood in bikini briefs in the shadow of the curtains. "I wonder what women wore...wear...underneath? I'll have to research it." The skirt slid easily over her hips. "My little canvas pumps are going to look ridiculous."

"I thought of that," Scott said. "There's a cobbler two doors down, but he won't be open till morning."

She smoothed the jacket and smiled. The fit was perfect. Turning to him, her smile faded; Scott was still wearing his silver belt buckle. And a gun. "Where did you get the holster?"

"I brought it with me."

"Why?"

"I told you, honey. Every man here carries a gun. If we're going to stay around old Tombstone, I have to dress accordingly." He smiled. "Hey, I'm a man. Men are just grown-up little boys, remember? I was a little cowboy who played Wyatt Earp games and wanted to be a big cowboy someday."

Sarah laughed. "And I was a little girl in love with a little gun-toting cowboy, and I thought it very daring and romantic."

"It's still daring and romantic . . . for us. Still a game. This is going to be great fun, my love!"

"How much did you get for the other gun?"

"Twelve hundred dollars."

Sarah gasped. "That much?"

"It was a gun that hasn't been invented yet—a snub-nosed, nickel-plated Smith and Wesson 38 revolver. Nobody's seen anything like it. If I'd had more than two boxes of shells, I could have held out for five thousand. But at least we've got money to get started on until I find work."

She looked again at the black leather holster. "Is that like the revolver you sold?"

"No, this is a new sixteen-shot semiautomatic Colt."
When she winced, he added, "I'm a collector. I told you,
I like target practice. And now we're here in the old
West. Indulge me."

Sarah knew little about handguns, but the word
"automatic" scared her. It meant he could keep on fir-
ing without recocking, and nobody else in Tombstone
could do that. No one on the frontier in the 1880s would
ever have heard of a semiautomatic pistol, either.

While they had been talking, Sarah had seen a few
performers running up and down the back stairs, to and
from what seemed to be a makeshift dressing room at
the back of the stage. There was still piano music, but
at the moment no act on stage. Scott took her hand and
led her down the front stairs into the theater itself.
Customers spoke to Sarah and called her Sparrow. Everyone knew her now.

"What is this 'Sparrow' business?" Scott asked as
they made their way past the gambling tables.

"I'll explain later."

She looked around for Josie and caught a glimpse of
her on the upper boardwalk, carrying a basket with a
whiskey bottle and glasses. Revulsion welled up; now
she began to understand what Josie's job entailed. How
terrible for a girl to have to live like this! But Josie
probably had no choice, had never had a choice.

They crossed the crowded saloon area and went out
the front door onto the covered wooden sidewalk. The
streets were crowded with men, many staggering—

compliments of too much whiskey. "Where are we going?"

"To find a place to stay. We'll try the Cosmopolitan Hotel."

"Isn't that where the Earps are supposed to be living?"

"That's right. I checked the date. It's the same day as we left, believe it or not. We rode that sorrel mare around the streets only yesterday."

"Yesterday! It's hard to fathom."

"It sure is."

A horse-drawn buggy clopped by as they crossed Fifth Street. Sarah brushed dust from her new skirt. The Cosmopolitan Hotel, in the next block, was well lit. They looked into the Crystal Palace Saloon; it had the same enormous bar that Sarah had seen the day before, when she'd walked alone down Allen Street in her jeans.

"It's hardly changed in all these years," she said.

"Actually the bar you saw yesterday is a replica. This, now, is the authentic one."

Sarah could hardly remember what places were still here in the 1990s. Not many of the commercial establishments, not the Wells Fargo office or the dozens of saloons on Whiskey Row.

"We've got to get you off this street," Scott said, quickening his step. "Or you'll be mistaken for a whore."

"In this beautiful outfit with a London label?"

"Decent women don't walk on this street. Especially at night. Remember?"

"I really care," she said flippantly, thinking how wrong her hairstyle was. Not even the "ladies of the night" wore their hair loose around their shoulders.

"Hey, come on. Get into the spirit. This isn't our time, Sarah." He was hurrying her as he spoke.

"I saw Josie," she remarked.

He grimaced. "So did I. On her way up to one of the cages." He paused to open the hotel door. "Here we are. If you'll wait here, my beautiful lady, I'll see what sort of accommodations they have for two tired travelers."

Tired? Who's tired? The quiet lobby was simply furnished, but the wood panels were polished to perfection. Oriental rugs covered the floor. There were other hotels, she thought in amusement. Scott wanted this one because the Earps were staying here. Well, perhaps that meant it was the best, and she had to admit that after years of reading about them, she wanted very much to see the notorious Earps herself. How many of her contemporaries had the chance to do *that?*

"We have a large room with a sitting area," Scott said when he rejoined her. "I had to say our luggage was lost. We're at the end of the hall upstairs with a window overlooking Allen Street."

Sarah blinked at him—at this man who was soon to become her lover. The lobby was hardly a place for a discussion about living arrangements, but it would have been proper and considerate for him to have consulted her. Once in the empty upper hall, she turned to him. "We didn't agree to stay together."

His eyes widened in surprise. "It never occurred to me you might object. You don't, do you?"

"I don't . . . know. It feels a little uncomfortable. We only met yesterday."

"We met twenty years ago, and you didn't have a problem with it then."

"Oh, well, if you sleep with your clothes on like you did then, I suppose I won't have a problem with it now, either." That was a lie. To sleep close to Scott would send her crazy with wanting him. Last night she hadn't slept for thinking about him. Why was she standing here in a cold hall in 1882, arguing about this? It was nothing more than a game; Sarah knew well and good that she was going to agree to the arrangement. She was just putting on a show and he probably knew it.

"We'll talk about it," he said gently. "I'll persuade you."

"Maybe that's what I'm afraid of."

"Never be afraid of me," he whispered in the quiet, dimly lighted hallway, touching her hair. "In all the world, in all times, I'm the one force you need never fear."

It was true. This man would give his life for her if he had to, and not just because it was the code of the West; he loved her.

He really loved her.

It seemed impossible, but he was still Lucky, and that boy had somehow committed himself as firmly to their love as she had. He was still Lucky. And he still loved her.

Scott turned the key in the lock and opened the door.

The room was nearly as cold as the night outside. In the light from the hallway, Scott found a kerosene lamp and lighted it with a match. The fact that he knew how intrigued Sarah. A soft, orange glow filled the room. Its furnishings were pleasant. A large bed and two dressers, and in a small alcove by the window stood a sofa, two chairs and a table. The curtains and bed-spread were of heavy brocade in shades of rose and gold and pink. There were lanterns on the table and candles here and there.

"I think this is the best Tombstone has to offer," Scott said. "Although the bathroom is down the hall."

"How exactly did you register us?"

"Lucky and Sally MacInnes."

She drew in her breath. "You did not!"

His eyes sparked with mischief. "Okay, not quite. I used Mr. and Mrs."

"We're married? When did this happen? I must have been looking the other way."

"It's either that or scandal. Besides, I saw how the men in the Bird Cage looked at you. I don't want any misunderstandings around here as to who you belong to."

Strangely, it sounded good, even right, for him to say that. Maybe up in the twentieth century it would sound chauvinistic, but things were different here; they could feel the difference in the very air they breathed. In this lawless frontier town with a thousand men for every woman, Scott was feeling responsible for protecting her. She welcomed his protection.

Clearly excited, he gave her a quick kiss. "We came here together, my love. We've come a long way together . . . further than anyone would ever believe. My life became part of yours once and I've never let you go. I belong to you as much as you belong to me."

She sat down on the edge of the bed, still trying to get used to this man, the stranger who was not a stranger. "It's a joint venture we've gotten ourselves into, all right. For the duration, whatever happens, we're stuck with each other."

Scott locked the door behind him. "I've waited for you most of my life, Sarah." He unbuckled his gun belt and set it carefully upon the dresser, just as he had done that night so long ago. This time he held out his arms afterward. "Here. Come here to me."

She rose without hesitation and fell into his waiting arms, and the weird world they had found came into focus.

Holding her, he said, "This is what I've been waiting for, a chance to be alone. We need time together to make sense of all this, to get to know each other...." He lifted her chin gently and kissed her; his kiss lingered and became part of the night and of memory. Memory and beginnings, fading and rising....

Sarah's breath left her and the unfamiliar room closed magically around them. Whether they belonged here or not didn't matter. They belonged together; that was all they knew.

His fingers caressed the back of her neck, under her hair, with slow, sensual movements—a message she couldn't misunderstand. The fingers moved on, along her neck, across her shoulders and down her spine.

"It's so soon...." she whispered.

"Twenty years isn't soon. I've waited so long."

"How could you, Scott?" She felt his heart beating against hers. "When you believed we would never see each other again?"

"Something inside me must have known we would find each other. I must have always known."

"I think I must have known, too. Because it was the same for me. Somehow I was always waiting for you to come back to me."

He lifted her hair and smiled. "My beautiful Sally. Real love lasts forever."

His hands moved over the buttons of her suit. He slipped off her jacket. Underneath she was wearing the thin turtleneck sweater.

"Will you lie down with me?"

"You sure don't waste time."

"I've wasted years of time. Now I want to know you as I never could before. We're not kids now."

She let him slip her narrow velvet skirt over her hips and watched him lay the new suit carefully over one of the chairs.

"Being kids was less complicated," she commented, pulling back the heavy bedspread.

"Not for me. I wanted you even then."

"You couldn't have!"

"I assure you, I did. I might not have known what it was all about, but I wanted you."

She kissed his forehead when he sat down on the bed again. The springs creaked under his weight. "You wouldn't have admitted it, though, would you?"

He laughed. "No. At eleven I had very strong convictions. I would never have touched you."

"And now?"

"Now you're a woman. And I'm a man."

"You are that. . . ." Sarah closed her eyes and luxuriated in the feel of the hands caressing her arms. His lips touched her throat.

He was a man like no other.

"This is the time for us, Sarah," he whispered. "These days and nights . . . this place . . . our secret . . ."

He slid the light sweater over her head and held her breasts in his hands. Warm, gentle hands. Large hands against delicate black lace. When he moved, she felt the shock of cold metal against her skin and jumped.

"Sorry," Scott said. "I should have remembered the buckle." He unsnapped it and pulled it out of the loops, saying, "Belt loops haven't been invented yet. I have the only belt-looped jeans in Tombstone."

"Really? How do you know?"

"The saleswoman at the shop where I bought your suit noticed my pants."

"Mmm. And I know why. They're also the tightest jeans in Tombstone."

"They're getting tighter by the minute."

Sarah's hands trembled on the buttons of his shirt, so much so that he had to help her. He tossed his shirt aside, pulled the white T-shirt over his head and struggled out of his jeans, then lay back on the bed, pulling her over him.

The sensation of his bare skin against hers sent her senses flying. He cradled her in his arms. "Are you cold, honey?"

"Not here, and not like this."

"We ought to have a fireplace. Winter nights are chilly." Caressing her shoulders, moving his hands to the clasp of her bra, he promised, "I'll keep you warm."

Her breasts fell free of their lace support. He tossed the bra aside and gently stroked her. Sarah caressed his dark hair, savoring his touch.

It was all strangely familiar, as if Scott had made love to her before. *I have dreamed this,* she thought. *Sometime, somewhere, I have dreamed this....*

She lay beside him in the soft glow of the lamp, enjoying the closeness. "I remember this scar on your wrist."

"Did I have it then?"

"Yes. I wondered what it was from."

"Barbed wire. You have a vivid memory, my sweet."

"I recall everything about you. The dimple in your chin, the cowlick in your hair. Your hair is darker than it used to be."

"Your hair's exactly the same. The color of wild honey."

Sarah's exploring fingers moved over his chest to his waist, his hard stomach. A man whose occupation involved hard physical exercise, his husky body was solid. When her fingers paused over the band of his briefs, Scott reached down and slipped them off.

"You memorized me as a boy," he said. "Now I want you to memorize me as a man." He closed his eyes. "Memorize me, Sarah. Your touch is like sunshine melting snow."

He was beautiful, but she would have loved him just as much if he hadn't been; Sarah couldn't have anticipated that the handsome boy she'd loved would develop so perfectly.... Even to look at his body, to touch him, was to live a fantasy. She felt less like the sunshine than the melting snow. "You are so tanned and yet you have no tan line," she mused. "Do you swim nude?"

He smiled, eyes closed. "When I'm alone, yeah."

Moaning involuntarily at her touch, Scott forced himself to lie back passively. He must seem different to her after so long. He must not overwhelm her with the intensity of his hunger. Responding to her need, he held himself back, to let her know him as he was now.

Sarah knew what he was doing and why, and loved him more for it. With each passing moment the song in her heart played louder, turbulent and beautiful, clamorous and tranquil, tormenting and rapturous . . . all emotions spun together in bewitching music. Music that was both love and desire.

As her fingertips traced the scar on his thigh, the memory flooded back . . . the flash of a knife blade in the sun, the scarlet rush of blood, Josie's steady hands, the glint of a needle. The neatly stitched L, swollen and frightening. Sarah moved her head to kiss the scar, allowing her tongue to trace it slowly and carefully, pausing at each small ridge left by the stitches. For protecting her, Scott was scarred for life. How many people—how many women—in bedrooms or beside swimming pools—had been curious about this scar and asked, but received no answer? Had he made up an answer? Someday she would ask him.

She explored his body, letting her lips follow her fingertips. *I have dreamed this*, the voice inside her whispered.

"Honey..." Scott rasped as if from somewhere far away. "You're making me...you're...I can't take much more of that...."

Holding him, Sarah shuffled until they lay side by side again and she could see his eyes. His eyes glowed feverishly. His kiss was burning hot, his tongue like flames.

His whisper was like an echo. "Sally..."

"I've seen your face in dreams," she whispered. "I've felt you touch me...."

His fingers felt hot on her skin, moving over her breasts, down her sides, over her hips as he slid away the last piece of lace. He traced every contour of her body as she had done, gently, like the tickling of an electric current. His hands took possession of her, and he whispered so softly she could barely hear, "You belong to me....

"Only to me." He moved his body over hers.

She moaned and trembled at the press of his body. Hands under her hips, he lifted her closer and closer, coaxing her into the rhythm of his body. The rhythm of his love. Slow at the start, like the first bubbling of a new and secret spring, then like springwater gushing, moving, joining a wild, falling brook . . . trembling, tumbling faster and harder, down and down and down.

Sarah fell into dreams. They had lived this before . . . loved before . . . joined before. . . . Somewhere his body had coupled with hers, even before tonight.

The dreams had to be magic, like his love.

She heard him cry her name.

"Sarah . . ."

He grasped her hands and held tightly while his body trembled violently.

Tears filled Sarah's eyes.

Propping himself on his arms, Scott gazed down at her. He smiled; he knew her tears were those of joy.

"My love," he whispered, leaning forward to kiss away the teardrops.

8

SHE WATCHED SCOTT SLEEP, remembering the tiny room in Nellie Cashman's hotel. Here in the dim light of this room she could see again the face of the boy she had loved for so long.

She touched him. He stirred and drew her close, as if they had slept together a thousand times before and he was accustomed to having her so near. Sarah lay in his arms, wrapped in a joy she had almost forgotten. She had found her love again!

Now he was a man, and he loved her. Hotly, crazily and deeply loved her.

Scott stirred again; his chest rose and fell in an enormous sigh. "Mmm. I didn't mean to fall asleep. It just sort of . . . happens to me. . . ."

"After you make love so feverishly?"

The way he made love, it was clear he knew a lot about pleasing women. Sarah wondered how many women there had been in his life. How many had he left because of a haunting memory of a little girl? She wondered, but didn't really want to know.

"Yeah." His voice was still sleepy. "I'm awake now, though. It doesn't last. I'm awake enough to make love to you again."

She snuggled against him. "I'm glad you want to spend these hours with me instead of whooping it up in that wild town down there, looking for some famous faces like Wyatt Earp's or Doc Holliday's."

"There's time. There's tomorrow. Right now I'm in bed with you."

"And it is a century ago. The real frontier is just outside that window."

He drew a finger along her chin and over her lips. "Maybe we should go have some dinner and see if we can find a decent bottle of wine in this town."

"I think this is a dream and tomorrow we'll wake up."

Scott stirred in the creaky bed. "It isn't a dream. We're really here. What incredible luck!" He caressed her shoulder as if he could not get enough of her.

She propped herself on one elbow. "Scott, earlier, when we left the Bird Cage, something was bothering you. What was it?"

He looked doubtful. "I'm not sure how I feel about your working at the Bird Cage. "It isn't safe."

"I couldn't turn down such a great job. Especially at that salary. It's my chance to earn some money here. It's a chance to be where I want for my research."

A shadow crossed his eyes. "Honey, the walls are full of bullet holes. You know how many murders take place there. The very air is tainted with sin. And all those love-starved, gawking miners and outlaws. It's not the sort of place I want the woman I love to be."

She sat up and studied him. "Scott, if we were living then...now...I could fully understand your attitude. Of course no man of the 1880s would want his woman at the Bird Cage. But we're not living then...."

He smiled at her. "Ah, but we are living then."

"No, we're not. Not really. We're only visiting. We're visiting to see what it was like. Nothing can change who we are or how we view things from our own perspective."

He didn't quite seem to agree. "But the point is we are here and we have to live as though—we have to fit in."

"I can fit in just fine, singing at the Bird Cage."

"A house of prostitution?"

"A theater." Her eyes challenged him.

Scott rubbed his chin, frowning, clearly not liking this.

"Scott," she said softly. "You tend to slide so completely into this century, this place. You did even as a child. And that's okay, that's fun. But we came here to learn, didn't we? And we're not staying long. Don't you see? I want to know about that place and those people. I want to mingle with them, just as you want to mingle with the gunfighters. We're not of this time, and I don't want to slip too far into it. It's different for a woman."

He scratched his head. "There are decent women in this town, but they stay away from Whiskey Row and the red-light district."

"You're getting to my point. How painfully dull their lives must be. I want the excitement, just as you do. I can be a decent woman next century. Here I'm the lover of a gun-toting cowboy. Hell, I'm not requiring *you* to be a model citizen during our stay. You have no intention of being respectable and we both know it." She rose from the bed and pulled the blanket away from him, wrapping it around herself and leaving him lying naked.

"Look," she said softly. She knew she had already made her point and he understood, but wanted to have her say, anyway. Scott didn't really know her and she wanted him to. "I'm not one of those women's rights fanatics or anything of the kind. I'm just your average 1990s working girl, trying to make a success of my career. I've been on my own since college. Nobody's been following me around, telling me what to do. The calendar on the wall over there might say 1882, but you and I are from the future and nothing can change that. I don't want my fun spoiled by having to stay on the respectable side of the street. And neither do you."

Now she saw mischief in his blue eyes. He reached out to touch her arm. "Honey, I was talking about the danger. I don't want anything to happen to you, because I love you."

"Nothing will happen to me. You're the one with the gun on his hip, remember?"

"I was trying to say you don't have to work to survive here. I'll support you."

"How?"

"I'll work on a ranch. It's what I've done all my life."

Sarah had expected something like this, but that didn't make it any less frightening. She had read enough about the history of Tombstone to know what a job as a ranch hand entailed. The word "cowboy" had come to be synonymous with rustler, so rampant was cattle theft. "You'll be right in the middle of the wars with rustler gangs!"

"It comes with the job. I'll check out the reputation of whatever ranch I hire on."

She blinked. "You *like* the excitement of shooting guns, I'll bet. And while you're chasing rustlers down to the Mexican border, what did you picture me doing? Sitting up here in this room, knitting shawls?"

"I hadn't got that far," he admitted. "I understand why you want to be where things are going on—at the Bird Cage. I guess I can handle it, if you can handle my tangling with rustler gangs."

"I hate the idea of your getting entangled in range wars. But okay. We're agreed. You're a ranch hand, I'm a singer and it's 1882."

He grasped her hand. "You're right. We don't know why we're here, so we'll just go with it."

Sarah slid down beside him, pulling the quilt over them, suddenly feeling guilty; he might be chilly, although he hadn't seemed to notice the cold. "I want to befriend Josie," she said.

"I wonder if you can. Josie is our friend, but she doesn't know it. In her world it was only this morning when she stitched up my leg. We can never tell her who we are."

"She's in trouble, Scott."

He nodded thoughtfully. "I know the business with Josie is unfinished. She was . . . is . . . in fear of her life. From what I've learned, prostitutes rarely have friends.

When I was lying on that cot I swore I'd help her because she helped us. I've always regretted not being able
to fulfill that vow."

Sarah shivered in disbelief. "Was it really only this
morning?"

"Yeah. The date is the same. We left today and came
back today."

"There was such a harshness in Josie's face tonight.
Yet only hours earlier she'd helped two runaway kids
because she knows what it is to be a kid in trouble."

"I caught just a glimpse of her." He rubbed his chin,
frowning at the memory. "Josie looks so young to me
now."

"She's only nineteen."

"And worldly in the worst sense of the word. You
started to tell me you saw something?"

"A man was strong-arming her and wouldn't let her
go. From a distance it looked like he was threatening her
and she was protesting. Just when I thought he was going to hit her, another guy stopped him. I think he didn't
want anyone paying attention to them, because afterward the two men sat at a table in a huddle. They were
obviously friends."

"He might have been a customer."

"I don't think she would have looked that frightened
of a customer. She would be used to dealing with ob-
noxious men. There was terror on her face. I'm sure it
was her husband."

"What'd he look like?"

"Really mean. Tough. A reddish beard. Maybe in his mid-thirties. It's hard to tell with all that hair on the face." A shudder of fear shot through her. "I need to find a way to befriend Josie."

"Yeah, maybe so. Maybe there is some way you can. And you can point out this bastard to me." Scott smoothed back her hair. "Why don't we send for some food? I don't feel like getting up again, and you don't have the proper shoes for going out."

"What are you going to do, phone down for room service?"

He pulled a face, sat up and reached for his clothes. "Hell, that's right. I'll have to go downstairs to order. No modern conveniences, except one—the twentieth-century lady in my bed, who rode in here on a song instead of a stagecoach."

THEY LAY AWAKE filling in years, getting acquainted again. He had been at the University of Arizona while she had been at the University of Southern California. He had been running his father's ranch, while she was taking acting classes to better understand the art of script writing. He had acquired his quarter horses while she was working out of a small apartment, making payments on a car, and making her first script sales. One summer he had gone skiing in Switzerland while she was skiing in Colorado. Both had had three relationships over the years with people whom they'd never been able to love deeply.

Finally she slept, curled beside him, and woke in his arms, knowing that was where she belonged. For the few days that they would be here, they would experience this adventure both together and in their own ways.

AT BREAKFAST, wearing her new suit, just-purchased high-top shoes and a hat that disguised her modern hairdo but made her feel ridiculous, Sarah sat across from Scott in the Maison Dorée, the restaurant next door to the hotel. Here they really were a part of the American frontier. Perhaps it was a combination of the morning calm, the normality of the day, the smell of coffee, the Arizona sunlight streaming in the windows of the dining room, and the sounds of voices around them.

"I'm curious about my great-great-grandfather," Scott said, stirring milk into his coffee. "He didn't buy his ranch until September of this year, which means he's probably out there prospecting the hills. He has to be in the valley someplace."

"How eerie to think about meeting your own ancestor!" The flowers on her hat annoyed Sarah; they were casting a lacy shadow over her eyes. Did women actually like these stupid hats? she wondered. Scott might; he was looking at her admiringly.

Several heads turned toward the entry as two tall men entered the Maison Dorée. One was blond, thin and gaunt, wearing a black coat that hung loosely on his frail frame. The other, also light-haired, was tanned and weather-beaten. They wore almost identical thick mustaches and short hair. And guns. They walked in as haughtily as if they owned the place and sat down at a corner table.

Sarah leaned forward. "The man in the coat is Doc Holliday! I recognize him from his pictures. Is he with one of the Earps?"

"Wyatt," Scott said, his eyes shining the way she remembered they had shone as a child when he'd first strapped the big pistol onto his belt. "I'm trying to look nonchalant and not stare, but my pulse is racing."

She, too, tried not to stare. "Wow! Wyatt Earp and Doc Holliday in the flesh, like they jumped out of one of your history books! Just imagine if they knew who *we* were! If they knew, we could tell them how long they'll live, when and where they'll die, and what people will say about them a hundred years from now!"

"It feels like some old movie turned real," he said. "I've wished a thousand times I could have got at least a glimpse of them when I was here before. Now it seems almost natural to be sitting here in the same room with a couple of my childhood heroes." He gulped his coffee, nearly dropping the cup because the handle was too small for his fingers. "It's funny how easy it is to adjust to a transition across time. It's starting to feel natural."

"I think it's easier for you. After all, Tombstone is where you've always lived. It doesn't seem all that natural for me."

He grinned. "How could it? You've attached yourself to the bawdiest bordello in the West . . . in the heart of a rough red-light district. Not exactly familiar ground."

She smiled back. "I've read so much about it, it seems familiar enough, but it does feel a bit . . . odd. I love the excitement of it, though!"

Scott was experiencing the same kind of excitement as he studied the two men who had sat down at the opposite end of the room to order breakfast. One a feared lawman, a fast gun, famous for gunfights, the other a onetime dentist turned gambler turned killer, who treated his tuberculosis with innumerable pints of whiskey and who throve on fights. Both men would outlive the boom days of Tombstone and both would die in bed.

"I've got to buy a horse," he said thoughtfully.

"And I've got to find a costume for tonight."

"What kind of costume?"

"Something appropriate for singing."

He stabbed a slice of bacon on his plate. "A long gown would be appropriate."

"Come now, you know better. A long gown would get me fired."

"All those drooling fools gaping at your legs."

She cocked her head. "You're doing it again, being old-fashioned."

"Since when is healthy jealousy old-fashioned?" He set down his fork. "Okay, I guess I am old-fashioned. I tend to think of you as an angel because of the mysterious way you appeared in my life. Almost as if you had come on the wings of a bird. I can't share that with the world, and I wish I didn't have to share you with a thousand lusting eyes. I can't help feeling that way. Besides, I grew up in a traditional world, much more old-fashioned than yours."

"You don't have to share me with the lusting eyes," she said gently. "What I'm wearing has nothing to do with anything."

"I suppose not," he conceded. After a silence he asked, "Do you need money?"

"Thanks, no. I have my own. I got an advance."

He squinted at that, dropped the subject and said, "I hate to leave you unprotected this morning, but if we're going to live here, I'll have to get out and find a fast, surefooted horse and get some tips on which ranch is hiring hands."

She wondered what they were in for, trying to fit in here, in an environment they neither knew nor fully understood. "Surely, kind sir, I don't need protecting in the middle of the day." Glancing across the dining room at the two aloof lawmen, she whispered, "They look mean as sin. You're dying to talk to them, aren't you?"

"Yeah. But I have no excuse...yet. Give me a few days to establish myself."

Sarah blanched. "I'm not sure I like the sound of that."

"You worry too much." He set down his napkin. "Shall we go? There's a lot to do today."

Sarah rose, aware that many men were staring. Though there were a few respectable women in Tombstone, not many ate breakfast on Allen Street, even though the Maison Dorée was a proper restaurant. She looked like a respectable woman this morning, too, with her velvet suit and lace sleeves and her hair in a bun hidden under the stupid hat. She wouldn't be respectable for long, though. The reputation of the Warbling Sparrow would spread fast. And Scott? Just how the devil did he intend to "establish" himself? While the adventure was fun they had to remember that Tombstone in 1882 was the most dangerous town in America.

She wasted two hours looking for a costume. The tailor's shop next to the Bird Cage wasn't open yet, and no other store carried anything even close. That surprised her when she recalled that "ladies of the night" in Tombstone numbered well over three thousand. Her miniskirt would have to do until there was time to try to sew up something—a depressing thought—Sarah knew she wasn't much good at sewing. Surely there must be a way to get her hands on some sequins or some gold brocade!

While she shopped, Sarah tried to figure out a way to approach Josie. She didn't feel comfortable inventing lies, but the truth would just not do.

The Bird Cage never shut its doors because the mines were open twenty-four hours a day, and miners headed for the saloons as soon as their shifts were over. It was nearly noon now. While the evening shows were the most extravagant ones, some form of entertainment also went on in the afternoon, and Sarah knew Josie was sometimes at the theater in the mornings. She had been yesterday.

Was it really only yesterday?

This time, an adult wearing her chic suit, Sarah entered by the front door. The bar was half-full, and she saw every head in the place turn toward her. *I work here*, Sarah kept reminding herself. *I have every right to be in here, whether these people think I look like I belong or not.*

Looking straight ahead, she walked to the end of the bar. When the bartender approached, she spoke brusquely, without smiling. "I'm looking for Josie. Is she here?"

He eyed her strangely. Hadn't he been on duty when she sang on stage last night? Didn't he recognize her? "Josie? I think she's here someplace, ma'am. Might be with a customer. I could give her a message for you."

"Thanks. I think I'll look for her myself." Little Josie Blue Eyes they called her. Josie was certainly one of the prettiest prostitutes in town—a dubious distinction—and perhaps one of the youngest. People—men—knew her.

Sarah saw Josie sitting alone at a table near the stage, eating a pastry and reading a tattered schoolbook. Beside her lay a pencil and a tablet with some lines written on the page. A half-filled tin coffee mug stood on the table.

Sarah took off her hat and, carrying it, hesitantly approached. "Are you Josie?"

The girl covered the tablet with one arm and looked up, squinting in the brightness. "Why are you asking?"

"I have a message for you from a kid named Sally."

The unfriendly gaze softened. Studying Sarah critically, Josie turned over her book. "What message?"

"Both Sally and Lucky are okay and they want you to know that. They also want to thank you for helping them. They asked me to find you and tell you."

Suspicion clouded Josie's face. "Where are they?"

"I met them at the train station in Benson on my way here. Their families caught up with them and took them home."

Josie considered this. "The families they ran away from?"

"They're nice people," Sarah insisted, desperately uncomfortable with her story. "The kids wanted to have an adventure, as I understand it. They wanted to see the Earps and a gunfight. Lucky wanted to be a cowboy and Sally came with him. It seems Lucky got himself in a bit of trouble while they were in Tombstone."

Josie looked so hard into Sarah's eyes that she grew uneasy. *She knows me!* she thought, then, *She couldn't, even if she saw a likeness.*

"How did they leave?" Josie asked. "He sure wouldn't have been riding a horse with that leg."

"I don't know," Sarah answered, glancing again at the book Josie had placed facedown on the table. It was a grammar school reader. She must be trying to teach herself. "I only know the kids talked about you and wanted to thank you and didn't get a chance. They said you saved Lucky's life."

"Hardly. I just stitched up a knife wound in his leg," Josie said dismissively. This wasn't the open, friendly girl Sarah had gotten to know yesterday. There was a hardness about her that young Sally had not seen.

"Lucky says he's coming back here to shoot someone," Sarah went on.

"What?"

"Something to do with you being in danger. He said he's going to run away again and come back here and shoot somebody to save you because you saved him."

Josie lowered her head. "How could he have heard?" she mumbled.

"They both heard something. Look," Sarah began, sliding back a chair and sitting down next to the younger woman. "It's none of my business, but if that boy shows up here again, be careful he doesn't get himself killed."

"He won't get too far on that leg." Josie took a sip of coffee.

Sarah pulled a package of chocolate mints from her pocket, popped one into her mouth, and offered another to the unsmiling woman who sat across from her. "Have one of these."

Josie accepted the chocolate without so much as a thank-you. "Are you the one who sang here last night?"

"Yes. I was offered the job, and just in time. Otherwise I'd be flat broke."

Josie chewed slowly, obviously savoring the delicacy. "I heard the song about the puppy in the window."

Her voice was whisper-soft and so sad that Sarah expected to see tears in the girl's eyes, but there were none, only a dullness. No sparkle whatever. Her heart went out to Josie. As if her life wasn't bad enough; now a sadistic bully was threatening her.

Sarah's thoughts seemed to have summoned him. The red-bearded man sauntered the length of the bar, across the room, then stood looking at them. She saw Josie glance up and stiffen.

"Who is that guy? I've seen him before. I think it was in Dodge City," Sarah lied.

Josie didn't answer, so Sarah decided to prod.

"Those eyes are evil. What is he looking at us for? Does he want something from you?"

Josie sat in silence, her face pale.

Sarah leaned closer. "Is he the one? The one who wants to harm you? The one Lucky heard you talk about?"

"Forget it," Josie answered coolly. "Why are you nosing into my business?"

"I'm sorry. It's just that those kids talked about you, about how nice you are. I hoped that maybe, since we both work here, you might be able to give me some advice. I have to find a costume or fabric to make one."

Sarah sensed that Josie was relieved to have someone sitting beside her; the man came no closer, but merely stood glaring.

"What does he want?" Sarah asked again.

Josie wouldn't look at him. She'd clenched her fists into tight balls. "Those kids," she said softly, ignoring Sarah's question. "Are you sure they're all right?"

"They're safe. And only unhappy about their special friend—you—being in some kind of danger. Kids have strong loyalties, at least these two have. Sally said you gave her a glass bird. It seemed to mean a great deal to her."

Josie's eyes fell. After a pause she said, "I might be able to help you with a costume. There's a place over in Hoptown that sells silks from China. I guess I could show you where it is. The tailor next door supplies a lot of our clothes here. He could cut and sew it."

Was Josie feeling genuinely more friendly now? Sarah wondered. Or was she grasping at an excuse to get out of here, away from the red-bearded threat? Putting out her hand, she smiled cordially. "My name is Sarah. I don't know a soul in town except my . . . my husband, who's looking for work on a ranch."

The younger woman closed her book and the tablet and dropped them carefully into a satchel; they were clearly treasured possessions. Picking up the cup and the half-eaten pastry, Josie said. "It's a rotten town you've come to. You'll wish you'd stayed away. Married to a cowboy, are you? All the cowboys I know are fighters. You'll soon wish you could leave, but you'll be trapped. That's how it is in Tombstone. You'll curse the day you ever saw this town."

Josie led the way, gliding past the red-bearded man without so much as a glance in his direction. Sarah saw him glare at them as they walked through the theater proper, but made no move to follow. A piano player had just seated himself at the huge instrument and was starting to pound out a bawdy tune.

They walked down Allen Street together on the side where respectable women didn't walk, heading for the Chinese settlement controlled by an indomitable woman known as China Mary. Josie seemed willing to talk about spangles and silk, at least. Sarah knew she had to be patient if she was to find out more about the danger Josie was in before it was too late.

A DEVIL WIND BLEW UP at about the time the cowboys rounded the hill, some five hundred yards from the watering hole that was fed by an underground spring. A devil's horn of dust whirled across the land like a minitornado. An omen of doom?

Scott rode with the men of the Double Bar Z toward the spring. Hiring on had been easy; good cowhands were always in demand, especially those who claimed to be handy with a gun. This land bordered the property his ancestor would buy, and many of the landmarks were just as Scott knew them. He felt at home, almost more so than he wanted to be. Sarah had been right; it was too easy to slide into the past because he knew much of it so well.

Suddenly they saw the silhouettes of men on horseback. Rustlers! Scott's heart pounded in his chest. The watering hole was the place thieves could always find cattle, and since Double Bar Z hands had ridden over this ground only yesterday, the rustlers probably didn't expect them to return so soon.

At the first sight of the intruders, the cowboys drew their guns and kicked speed into their horses.

Cornered, the rustlers opened fire. The cowboys fired back.

Scott didn't target anyone in particular. The air of unreality still surrounded him, making it more of a game than reality—Lucky's kind of cowboys-and-rustlers game.

The horses kicked up more dust and the wind blew it into the men's faces, making their eyes sting. Through the swirling dust Scott saw one of the rustlers cut around a cluster of scrub oaks. Scott followed and saw the outlaw take careful aim at a Double Bar Z hand called Billy Gray.

Gunshots ran out. Seconds later, the rustler, not Billy Gray, lay dead.

Scott lowered his right arm. His hand was surprisingly steady. There hadn't been time to think, only to react. A moment's hesitation on his part would have cost Billy his life. But Scott's presence had changed the course of history for at least two people, and this realization numbed and subdued him. Later, riding back, Scott felt a weakness in his knees, queasiness in his stomach. The gun at his side was more enemy than friend. For the first time it felt unnatural as hell to be carrying a weapon.

BY LATE AFTERNOON the Bird Cage Theater was jumping. In one of the "bedrooms" below the stage, Josie was helping Sarah put the finishing touches of her costume, a simple, pale pink shift with fringes and a very short skirt that the tailor had sewn up in a couple of hours. The fringes moved with Sarah's body. The silk would shine in the bright spotlights.

"I appreciate your help," she said. "I couldn't have done this without you." Watching Josie sew a few fake pearls at the neck, she remembered her stitching the wound in Scott's leg.

"It's okay," Josie answered. "It was just as well I walked around Hoptown today—at least got myself out of here."

"Why do you say that? Because of that man who was staring? I saw him manhandle you yesterday, Josie. What does he want from you?"

Josie swallowed hard and finally answered, "My life. Also my money, what little I have."

"Tell me why. Maybe I can help."

"No one can help. I belong to him. I'm married to him, which means he owns me."

"He doesn't! There are laws. . . ."

Josie looked up from her sewing. "There are? Laws to protect women? What laws?"

Sarah abruptly remembered where she was. "Hell, maybe there aren't laws here to protect women. There don't seem to be many laws here at all." She tried to meet Josie's lifeless eyes. "Does he really mean to hurt you?"

Josie nodded slowly. Her jaw was set. In anger? Fear? Both? "Yes, he means to punish me for running away from him." She seemed unable to look at Sarah, saying softly, "You're right, you probably did see him in Dodge. I was in Dodge before I ran off and came down here. A lot of people who got in trouble in Dodge City came down here."

"So he followed you. . . . How did he know where to find you?"

A shaky shrug. Helplessness? "I don't know. Maybe he only guessed. Somehow, though, after he got here, he found out I was making good money. So he apparently decided I should live a little longer. That way he can get money out of me. But he keeps saying he can kill me anytime. And he will." Her voice cracked. "He'll kill me as soon as I'm no use to him anymore."

Sarah both saw and felt the other woman's fear. She'd been so reluctant to talk at first, and then it had come pouring out. How lonely her life must be! "I'm glad you decided to tell me," Sarah said softly. "Maybe there's some way I could help."

Josie shook her head. "I don't see how. It's just a matter of time. I'm as good as dead unless I outsmart him." She looked up from the pink silk and Sarah saw her eyes change mysteriously. "Maybe I'll do just that."

"How?"

"First off by stalling. I—" She stopped and fell silent.

"Tell me, Josie. I guess you're not used to talking about your problems, but tell me, anyhow. You need to get it out. You can trust me."

"I know I can trust you, because you befriended Sally, too. You know, Sarah, you remind me awfully much of her. You're so like her, the way you laugh. Even the dimple in your cheek when you smile. It's amazing. Maybe that's what makes me comfortable around you. I keep thinking I know you. I liked Sally. I wish she could have stayed longer, but then if she had, I guess I couldn't have seen her again. Nellie wouldn't have let her associate with the likes of me." Josie's voice had grown more animated, her eyes brighter. Some of the stiffness in her shoulders had disappeared.

"What did you mean, you might outsmart this guy. . .this husband?" Sarah asked.

Josie bit off the thread with her teeth and studied her handiwork. "Charlie . . . that's his name. Eagle Charlie they call him because he's killed so many eagles. He's not really my husband, but he claims he is. Claims I married him in Dodge and he has some fake paper to prove it. He's a scum who lives off a woman's wages, and his word is believed instead of mine because he's a man and I'm . . . who I am." Her tone grew angry. "Charlie found out one of my customers works for Wells Fargo and got it into his head that I could find out when the next payroll shipment comes into Tombstone from the Benson railroad. He wants to steal the payroll."

"Are you thinking of giving him the wrong information?"

"If I do, he'll kill me."

"Do you know when the stage is due?"

"I'm not saying. I'm only saying he thinks I know and as long as he thinks so, I'm alive."

They heard loud voices from the room where the poker game was going on. Josie walked to the door and peered out. Sarah followed. Through the thick smoke they could see men standing around the table, talking.

"What's the chatter about?" Josie called to the two nearest. "What's happened?"

"A shooting on the Double Bar Z," one answered. "A rustler was killed a couple hours ago. Some cowboy who'd been working for Frank Botts less than three hours done it. This stranger can fire a gun faster than anybody they ever seen, the men are saying. His name is MacInnes."

Sarah felt her heart drop into her stomach. *Scott had killed a man?* After only one day?

9

FULL MOON ABOVE MY SHOULDERS. How does that song go?

"Tonight the moon is full," Sarah told her audience between numbers, trying to give herself time to decide what song to select next from the hundreds she knew. "Be careful of white horses running away under the full moon."

Her remark referred to a Tombstone incident she had read about. A team of white horses, pulling a wagon, frightened by gunshots, had run along Allen Street and run into a sheriff's deputy, nearly killing him. For some reason the horses' behavior had been blamed on the full moon, still high in the sky that winter sunrise.

Sarah had discovered she was a natural performer. The rowdy miners, cowboys and lawmen crowded into the theater to see this mysterious woman in the short skirt who sang songs unlike any they had ever heard. The pianist, an expert improviser, was delighted, too.

She thought of old country songs, rock songs and movie themes. If any of those she sang caught on and were remembered, though, it could cause problems for their writers, people yet to be born.

But Scott had already changed history in a far more serious way. He had killed a man.

She spotted him in the audience. Now he was a rider for the Double Bar Z—wherever the hell that was—he was surrounded by other cowboys, all drinking. Scott watched her every move without smiling. The sight of him frightened her; he looked as though he belonged here. Lucky had looked for a place where he might fit into this dangerous mining community; Scott had found it.

She took a final bow before a hail of applause, walked off the stage and into the audience. Scott stepped forward to meet her and drew an arm possessively around her waist.

"I hope you never have to bend over in that getup," he said. "But your voice is beautiful. You can captivate the world the way you captivated me."

"But you don't want me to. You weren't smiling while I was singing."

"I'd rather you sang only to me."

"I will, then. I do. Never mind who else is eavesdropping." She paused to straighten a strap of her costume. "Rumors are all over town, Scott. You didn't actually kill a rustler?"

He squeezed her tighter. He must have downed several beers, but his voice was clear. "'Fraid I did. It was either the rustler or Billy Gray. I had no choice but to shoot."

Something in his voice was telling her, *It wasn't really that simple. Killing a man wasn't easy.* But he wouldn't say it outright, she knew that.

"And shoot damned fast, this fella did!" drawled one of Scott's companions. "Never saw a man draw a gun as quick. Never saw a gun like this. People's talking about it all over town."

Sarah looked from one smiling face to the next. "Well," she said to Scott. "You said you were going to establish yourself. You sure wasted no time."

"Circumstances," he insisted, accepting another beer from a newfound pal. "We took the rustlers by surprise. Johnny Ringo was in that gang. He rode off shooting, but not before I met him eye to eye. I didn't even known who he was until somebody told me later. Ringo has the eyes of a killer." He took a swig of the ale. "So did the rustler who had Billy in his gun sight. It's lucky for Billy I was there."

I think, Sarah thought, *that he is trying to convince himself of that more than he is trying to convince me.*

BEFORE DAWN the next morning while the full moon sat high in the western sky, two white horses pulling a wagon full of firewood were startled by gun shots near Allen and Sixth. Opposite the theater, a deputy walking in front of the general store was hit by the run-away horses as he stepped into the street. The deputy was rushed to Doc Goodfellow's office with a bleeding head wound.

Every person who set foot on Allen Street that day heard the same story: the new singer at the Bird Cage, the Warbling Sparrow, was a fortune teller, a seer of the future.

Sarah had not realized that her words onstage were a prediction—the runaway horses hadn't yet taken place. As a result, today people were clamoring for appointments to have their fortunes told. This was too good a money-maker to pass up; after all, both she and Scott knew a great deal about Tombstone's future. So with a deck of ordinary playing cards for props, she went into the fortune-telling business at a charge of a dollar a throw.

Scott spent the day chasing and bringing in two wanted bandits. From the history books he knew that the robbers of the Tar Baby saloon on the edge of town had been found at a stage post, trying to steal two horses. The Tar Baby had been held up just last night. Since there was a bounty on the heads of the thieves, he rode out to the post, held the villains at gunpoint and brought them in.

Wyatt Earp himself came out to shake Scott's hand, and by late afternoon the whole town was buzzing about the captured thieves and the fast-gun cowboy MacInnes. Yesterday he had outdrawn the rustler, today he was collecting bounty money on two robbers.

Just after twilight, pleased with himself because he was now playing an active role in Tombstone's war against bandits, just as he had done in all his childhood fantasies, Scott walked with Wyatt Earp into the Bird Cage. There they learned that the Warbling Sparrow had become the most popular woman on Allen Street; she could predict the future! He and the deputy marshal, ordered one beer after another and watched her sing "Red River Valley" and "Mamas, Don't Let Your Babies Grow up to Be Cowboys," while the crowd went wild.

The two men were joined by Morgan and Doc Holliday who were interested in finding an open poker game because they couldn't get into the one under the stage.

"We're headed for Hatch's," Wyatt told Scott. "Want to come along?"

"I'll stay," Scott said, leaning on the bar. "Got to keep an eye on my lady."

Soon after they left, a fight broke out in the line of people waiting to have their fortunes read. A mob of prospectors had converged on the theater, wanting to learn from the Sparrow whether or not they would get their silver strikes. They kept Sarah so busy she scarcely noticed Scott.

Disgruntled, he left the crowded bar and walked onto the street; maybe he should meet the Earps and Doc Holliday, after all. The moon was beginning to rise. The noise from the saloons drowned the familiar night sounds from the valley and the hills—the soft wind and the howl of coyotes that were sounds of peace for Scott.

He felt unsettled. This wasn't exactly the way it was supposed to be. Sarah was already so involved in the Bird Cage, she had become *part* of the place. She was actually willing to let herself be ogled and shouted at, pursued and fought over by a bunch of ruffians and outlaws! She'd even called it fun! Adventure! She was associating with prostitutes, living in their world, perhaps being taken for one. Research was one thing, but this was going too far.

He, on the other hand, cared what people thought. Sarah was the most beautiful woman in town. And she was his. She didn't belong in this sad, tainted world. Enough was enough.

Scott was already used to the feel of his gun on his hip. Endless hours, no, years of target practice—he had won three championships—were paying off. If a guy had a chance to live in the wild days of the frontier, then he should be a part of the place and the time. He should make a name for himself.

But a woman? That was different.

The gentle sex represented the gentle side of living. A woman represented dignity and softness. His head was so full of what he had seen at the Bird Cage—men pushing and shoving and fighting to get to Sarah—that Scott walked the covered wooden sidewalk of Allen Street, not thinking of the dangers in the shadows.

Without warning, a man jumped in front of him, brandishing a gun and yelling, "You're the next corpse for Boot Hill, MacInnes. We got no use for bounty hunters in this town."

Scott had known he was taking a chance when he went after the bounty for the thieves, but hadn't expected so quick a response. He knew he had no time to draw; the other man's hand was already on the trigger. When the sound of a gunshot filled the night, he expected to feel the fire of the bullet in his chest, but felt nothing. Instead, the gunman howled, buckled, and went down kicking, his gun arm spurting blood.

The stranger who had fired was standing a few feet away. To Scott's surprise he was dressed like a miner, not a cowboy; he walked toward the wounded man without a second glance at Scott.

"We got no use for cold-blooded killers in this town, either," he said in an odd accent, picking up the wounded man's gun. The gunfire had brought a crowd to the street. The miner told the first to arrive to fetch Doc Goodfellow. Then he backed away and stepped into the shadows.

Scott was right behind him, but the stranger didn't stop until he was around the corner, beside the Oriental Saloon.

"Hang on!" Scott demanded. "You saved my life back there. Give me a chance to say thanks."

The miner turned toward him. In the dim light the blue eyes looked pale in the clean-shaven, handsome face under the shadow of the broad-brimmed hat. He couldn't be more than twenty-two.

"I saw he wasn't giving you a chance to draw." The accent was pure Scots.

Scott held out his hand. "My name's MacInnes."

The blue eyes looked directly into his. "I know who you are. And I heard you were asking after me, so I was about to ask you why, when this bloke moved in on you. We aren't related, if that's your question. I've got no relatives, not in America."

Scott stared, his mind racing.

"I'm Ian MacInnes," the miner said, not offering his hand.

Ian MacInnes. His great-great-grandfather had just saved his life! Scott felt dizzy.

"Are you okay, mister?"

Scott nodded, still trying to absorb this. Ian MacInnes!

"I can't think why you'd be asking about me around town unless you thought I was somebody else. A relative, maybe?"

"Uh . . . yeah," Scott replied, grasping at the straw. "A relative who came out here prospecting."

"I don't know another MacInnes. If he was working the Dragoons, he might or might not still be alive. The Apache war parties have been busy out there."

Scott wished he could tell this young Scotsman face-to-face that he was his great-great-grandson...wished he could tell him he was going to hit a hell of a rich strike before the middle of next summer and become one of the most respected landowners in the Arizona Territory. . . .

"You've been prospecting the Dragoons?" Scott asked his ancestor.

"How'd you know I'm prospecting?"

"I—I heard it. When I was asking around. I didn't expect to find you. Didn't think you'd be in town."

"I came in to see my girl."

His girl? Who might that be? Eligible young women were almost nonexistent in Tombstone. How could a poor miner possibly attract one of the elite few, even with his good looks?

"Are you getting married?" Scott asked, realizing too late how out of line his curiosity must sound.

"At present I'm a man with no home, not even a very good horse. When I find the silver, aye, then, maybe. Give her a better life than the one she's got now at the theater." He shifted, clearly impatient. "Nice meeting you, MacInnes. I hear you're fast with your gun. You'll have to look into the shadows so you won't be a target for the next idiot who fancies himself a faster draw than you. Mind your back." He turned away.

"Are you heading for the mountains?" Scott wanted to know.

"Aye, I am. I've got to get some supplies and be on my way before sunup."

If there was a way to stay longer in this man's company, Scott wanted to find it. "Hey, I owe you my life. At least let me buy you a bottle of whiskey. . . ."

"That's not necessary. I just happened to be on the spot . . . this time." He settled his shallow-crowned hat more firmly on his head and smiled almost sadly, clearly believing the older man's days were numbered. The fast guns were a target for every want-to-be from Dodge City to Tombstone. You were only somebody if you could outdraw the fastest.

Scott MacInnes knew this.

Apparently so did Ian.

NOT TO MENTION SARAH. Fear and worry were already a burden. Scott had willingly put himself in danger because he loved the whole stupid idea. Gunmen of the Wild West! Did men never grow up? If he could kill, here in the past; if he could change history, then he could also *be* killed.

She found him in the bar, waiting to escort her home. "It's pretty damned late," he complained.

"I did three shows tonight besides the fortune-telling. It works better doing three short shows than two longer ones. There's also a juggler on the program and a trapeze artist, and tomorrow a dance troupe from Ireland."

He was unusually quiet during the walk to the hotel. Sarah could get nothing out of him.

Once in their room, he watched her take off the dark gray skirt and white blouse she'd bought that morning.

"Why did you leave the theater tonight?" she asked.

"I can't stand all the unwashed, filthy-minded fools drooling over you. We have to talk, Sarah. This can't go on."

She unpinned her hair and shook it free. "Oh, but the theater's so stimulating! It literally vibrates with sin! Did you know the 'painted women' have thirty-six-inch-wide double portable benches that they take up to the cages when a man hires them? He buys a token at the bar for twenty-five dollars, and that gets him a bottle and a girl, with her folding, upholstered bench that just fits into the cage. They just pull the curtains and . . ."

"I know what goes on there." He scowled. "I'm not blind. What's so stimulating about it?"

"The naughtiness of it all! The atmosphere! I'm keeping a journal. What a fabulously authentic atmosphere for my—"

"Okay. You've seen the Bird Cage. Now you can write about it. Tell Hutchinson tomorrow will be your last day."

She blew up. "I might consider it when you put your gun away!"

"I can't do that."

"Why not?"

"For one thing, if I don't carry it now, I'll get shot. I almost did tonight. My great-great-grandfather saved my life."

Sarah was brushing her hair. She stopped, surprised. "What? You met him?"

"Some fool on the street would have shot me if he hadn't been there and intervened. Makes you stop and think, doesn't it?"

Her heartbeat quickened. "What is he like?"

"Young, good-looking, pale eyes like mine. Scottish accent. He's been in the hills prospecting, as I suspected, and going back up there tomorrow, so I might not get a chance to see him again."

"That's exciting, Scott! Didn't you wish you could tell him he would make his strike?"

"Yeah." He paused, hesitant to tell her what else they had talked about. "He said he came in to get supplies and see his girlfriend."

"Really? Could she be your—?"

"No, she couldn't. He said she works at the theater. I have to assume he meant the Bird Cage, because that was obviously where he'd been." He paused as he began to understand what this implied. "Anyway, he left after a minute or two. We didn't talk long enough for me to learn anything about him except that he didn't . . . doesn't . . . have much regard for gunfighters."

"Your ancestor sounds like an honorable man. I wonder who his girlfriend is."

"Who knows? He probably just has a favorite."

Slipping her new white cotton nightgown over her head, Sarah asked, "How old do you think he is?"

"Early twenties." He paused again. "What is that thing?"

"My nightgown."

"What do you need a nightgown for?"

"Good heavens, Scott. You want me to be a woman of the times. Women of the 1880s have to have nightgowns."

"You don't know that."

"Of course I do."

"Take off the white tent and come here."

"I'm not sure that would be authentic."

He laughed. "I'll show you what's authentic."

"I'll hold you to that." This time she did as he asked, pulled off the gown and climbed into bed beside him. The room was chilly, but the bed was warm. He felt so good; she sighed contentedly and lay down beside him.

"Josie knows when the Benson Stage is bringing in the payroll for the mines," she muttered.

He stroked her hair. "I thought you weren't sure she knew the actual schedule."

"She knows. I'm sure now. The Wells Fargo man saw her again last night. The shipment is easily worth a hundred thousand dollars. That creep Eagle Charlie is determined to force her to tell him the date, and she's so scared of him I think she might do it. There's no telling what he'll do to make her talk, Scott!"

He caressed her shoulder, listening with little enthusiasm. "Get her to tell you when the shipment is due."

"I tried. She won't."

"Try again. Then I'll go after Charlie and catch him in the act."

"That's dangerous!"

"Not a bit. I've got the only semiautomatic pistol in town, remember?"

"How could I forget? Everybody's talking about your gun. A hundred men are probably planning to kill you for it."

"Mmm," Scott murmured, no longer interested in anything to do with Eagle Charlie. "Your skin is soft. I've never felt skin as soft as yours."

She closed her eyes, luxuriating in his touch as his hands gently, sensually explored her body.

"They look at you with their imaginations," he said.

Her hands moved in slow circles across his hard chest. "Oh? And I suppose you pretend not to notice the

way women look at *you* in those tight jeans. It's dis-
graceful. Is your ancestor as handsome as you?"

"I look like him. I don't suppose he would have seen
any resemblance between us. It was damned
strange...." His voice faded and his hands began to
caress her breasts. After a while he whispered, "Everything else goes away when we're alone together, like
this.... I realize how much I've missed you all my life.
Never leave me again, Sarah."

"I don't want to leave you. I belong with you. But I
don't belong here."

He kissed her softly and time went away. The cold
room seemed to grow warm. The fears of the day dis-
solved like the morning mist. Two people suspended in
time. They were all that mattered.

She kissed his throat and chest, and her fingertips
found the scar on his thigh again, a wound now as familiar to her touch as to her memory.

"Your touch is magical," he whispered and shifted
onto his back. "Take away the space between us, Sarah.
Lose yourself in me. Make love to me."

NEXT DAY she was nervous and distracted. Josie came
in early with black-and-blue bruises on her arms. Sarah
suspected she was spending so much time at the theater because she was safer there than at home, a shanty
among the row of cribs on Sixth Street, the red-light
district. Eagle Charlie was evidently using force to try
to persuade Josie to reveal the date of the payroll shipment.

Coffee and fresh raspberry pastry in front of her, Josie sat at the same back table as before. She was writing something when Sarah approached and didn't look up.

"Mind if I join you?" Sarah asked.

Josie motioned toward the empty chair and Sarah sat down. "You look pretty busy."

"I'm writing a poem. I like writing poems. I've done twenty-four of them."

"That's terrific!"

"For a girl who never went to school, it's pretty good. I taught myself to read and write. I'm not real good, but I'm getting better. My poems aren't spelled very good."

"Poems are an art form. Spelling doesn't matter. What do you write about?"

"Just things...how the trees look when the leaves are wet with rain and then the sun comes out. How spiders spin their webs. I like watching spiders spinning webs. When the wind blows in dust and leaves, the spider cleans them all up and respins, so they'll be perfect again. Webs are so beautiful in the rain. Don't you think so?"

Sarah nodded. This girl across from her was really sensitive to the subtle wonders of the world, but the veil of sadness never left her eyes. Would it ever? "Are you writing about a spiderweb now?"

"No, it's a love poem for someone. Do you want to see it?"

Sarah reached for the tablet.

Yours is a misty, distant land.
Strange, dark tales you tell.
I, too, have come from far away
. . . as far away as hell.
You do not ask where. You find my soul,
Your eyes that love me know me well.

Tears sprang to her eyes. "Who is he, Josie?"

"Just . . . someone. . . ."

"Does he know about this awful business with Charlie?"

"Heavens, no! I could never tell him about Charlie. I got mixed up with that maggot because I owed a friend of his some money. He's clung to me like a bloodsucking leech ever since, claiming we're married because I make pretty good money."

"But this man—the one your poem is for—maybe he could help you, Josie."

Her face grew even paler. "No. It's bad enough. . . No, I don't want him to find out about Charlie."

"But how can he not? I don't think you got those bruises falling downstairs." Sarah leaned closer. "Let Scott help you, Josie. He could make short work of Charlie."

I can't believe I just said that, Sarah thought. *I'm losing my hold on reality just as surely as Scott is.* Her fear for Josie's life must be making her desperate. Just what did she think Scott should do to Eagle Charlie at the holdup? Shoot him? Hand him over to Marshal Earp for hanging?

The girl smiled. "Your Scott is a dangerous man. I'll think about it."

"You haven't told Charlie the stage schedule, have you?"

Josie shook her head.

Suddenly angry, Sarah pounded the table. "Can't you go to the marshal about this?"

Josie laughed bitterly. "Not if I want to live until tomorrow."

This is Tombstone, Sarah reminded herself. Josie was right. A common prostitute, one among thousands here, she felt she had no rights, and in truth she probably hadn't. She handed back the tablet. "I like your poem very much."

"Thanks. I like it too. It's my best one." Josie tore it out, folded the paper carefully, and pushed it into a pocket of her dress.

Scott has to help Josie, Sarah thought. Josie's life was in peril. Scott would have to figure out a way to get rid of Eagle Charlie—hopefully short of killing him.

SCOTT HAD READ ABOUT the robberies of the Sandy Bob and the Benson stages. The payrolls for the Tombstone and Bisbee mines had been taken more than once, but he couldn't exactly remember when the Benson stage robberies took place. So many shipments had come in. The chief Wells Fargo detective, James Hume, coming to investigate the rash of robberies, had himself been a victim, his pistols stolen, when the stage bringing him into Tombstone was held up.

Scott couldn't call the cards on this one; he simply didn't know if the particular stage Charlie wanted to rob had in fact been stopped by thieves.

Tomorrow night he would pick a fight with Charlie in the Bird Cage. If the guy was stupid enough to pull a knife or a gun, he'd have an excuse to do him in permanently. If not, he could beat him badly enough to disable him until after the stage run. The shipment was expected sometime within the next thirty hours.

He waited for Charlie at the Bird Cage, but the man didn't show up. Scott was surprised at his own disappointment. He was finding it easy, perhaps too easy, to live out his role as a tough guy like Wyatt and Doc and the other characters of Tombstone—men other men feared.

Josie had shown compassion and concern for two helpless children once, and he had vowed to save her from the man who was threatening her life. Eagle Charlie wasn't safe, as long as Scott MacInnes was in town, and sooner or later Charlie was going to learn this. The hard way.

SO DID two masked bandits. Clouds covered the waning moon. The night was so black that the scrub oaks and palo verdes could barely be seen in silhouette against the sky. The clopping rhythm of running horses and the creak of wooden wheels broke the silence as the stage approached from the direction of Benson.

The coach had just left Contention, eight miles northwest of Tombstone. Standing near a clump of bushes, the bandits fired into the air, then rode in front of the wagon, six-guns waving. They shot the guard and took the two Wells Fargo money boxes.

More shots ran out as the robbers rode off. One of the bandits dropped the box he was carrying, hit the ground and lay as still as death. The second, in fear of his life, also dropped a box while bullets whizzed past his head, then used the darkness to get away.

A figure appeared, dismounted, collected the money boxes, and strapped them over the saddle. The gunman rode away.

10

SARAH HAD JUST CHANGED out of her costume and removed her stage makeup in the washroom under the
stage when she caught a glimpse of a figure entering
through the back door. Poker players used this door
regularly, particularly for the community outhouse just
outside, but this was not a poker player. Wearing dark
pants, black jacket and a hood, it hurried past the poker
game without a glance and made for the washroom
Sarah had just vacated.

Beneath the stage of the Bird Cage Theater were two
finely decorated "bedrooms" that rented for forty dollars a night, including whiskey and a woman. There
was also a well-stocked wine cellar. Near the stairway,
behind a railing, the seven-player poker game went on
twenty-four hours a day. Scott had told her there was
a thousand dollar buy-in and a list of people wanting
in at the first opportunity. He had also told her that,
according to history, the poker game had lasted eight
and a half years. The house did the dealing for a ten-
percent cut.

The hard-faced cardplayers were too intent on their
game to notice either her or any other of the Bird Cage
employees coming and going nearby, unless they were

bringing whiskey. Cigar smoke hung so thick it burned her eyes.

Passing the dark-clad figures, Sarah caught a glimpse of the face behind the hood. Startled, she said softly, "Josie?"

The girl looked up at her in surprise and the hood fell back, revealing her light hair, which was tied back in a bun. Josie quickly ducked inside the small washroom. Sarah followed and closed the door.

"Why are you dressed like that? Where have you been? I thought you were upstairs . . . working."

"I've been out," Josie answered briskly. "It's raining."

"Is something wrong?"

Josie smiled a strange smile. "Nothing is wrong. Everything is absolutely fine."

The sadness that had always dulled Josie's eyes was gone. For the first time Sarah saw the blue eyes sparkle with life. Something *had* happened. Something good. Yet Josie gave off unsettling vibrations, hints of joy and fright at the same time.

"I'm going to change and go on upstairs," Josie said. "Are you finished singing early?"

"I always finish around two o'clock."

Josie pulled off the hood and tucked it under her arm. "I didn't realize it was so late. I'll see you tomorrow, then."

Sarah hesitated. "Josie, something has happened."

"I won't deny it." Josie smiled again. "I've now found a reason for living."

Ah, Sarah thought. She's been to meet her lover. She's ridden into the night and met him in secret, so his friends wouldn't know he was involved with one of the Allen Street girls. Josie must be in love.

Scott wasn't waiting to walk her home, as she had hoped. The night was cold, and rain was beating upon the wooden roof of the sidewalk as she hurried along under the gaslights, feeling more afraid of being alone at night than she would ever have admitted to Scott. Near the hotel the tall form of Morgan Earp came out of the Cosmopolitan and walked toward her. He touched the brim of his hat and nodded as they passed.

Morgan smiled. He was the youngest and best looking of the brothers, and he would be the first to die. Soon. Sarah shuddered. His death would lead to more murders and result in all the Earps and Doc Holliday leaving Arizona for good.

She knew she shouldn't change history, but the hard part was, it didn't seem like history now. These were living, breathing people, not names in a book. Morgan Earp was a man smiling at her on the street. He was too young to die.

Scott wasn't in the room, either. Sarah slipped on the white nightgown and snuggled under the blankets for warmth, but there was no hope of sleeping without knowing where Scott might be in the middle of the night. She lay staring into the darkness, wondering about Josie's secret lover, wondering what Eagle Charlie would do if he found out about this man. Her thoughts wandered again to the impending death of

Morgan Earp. There had to be a way to warn him; she was supposed to be a seer, after all. Should she warn him and change the whole history of Tombstone?

Scott came in just before 3:00 a.m. with mud on his boots, the shoulders of his leather jacket dark with rain. He moved quietly, thinking she was asleep.

"You've been out in the rain," she said.

He was sitting on a chair in the alcove by the window, pulling off his jeans. "The Benson stage carrying the payroll was held up tonight. One thief got away. The other was killed—apparently by his partner, who didn't want to share the money. The dead man had a red beard."

Sarah sat up in bed. "The money was stolen? All of it? And Charlie was killed holding up the stage?"

"I don't know for sure it was Charlie. I was riding with a posse searching for the thief."

Josie must have told Charlie. And he'd gotten himself killed because of it. Where had Josie been tonight?

"Morgan wasn't with you," she said. "I saw him on the street a while ago."

"Nobody could find him, and we were trying to get out of town before the trail was too cold." Scott folded his jeans over a chair and unbuttoned his shirt.

"I take it the posse wasn't successful."

"No. It's so dark out with the rain. Daylight might give us some clues as to where the other guy rode with both payroll boxes." Naked, he dropped into bed beside her.

"That means you're riding with the posse again tomorrow?"

"They can use another fast gun. I've been trying to place this particular holdup in history but I can't. I remember there were three where the stolen money was never found, and this might be one of them. But with my gun and fast horse, I might be able to do what the others couldn't . . . find Eagle Charlie's partner and murderer *and* the money."

Sarah touched his bare shoulder. "You fit right in here and you're proud of it."

"On the frontier the gun is the only law. It's the code of the West."

"Oh, for Pete's sake! The code, as you call it, is barbaric!"

He grunted. "In some ways it makes more sense than the way we live now."

"Makes more sense for whom? Not for women. I've been talking to a few of the prostitutes. They won't reveal much about themselves, but one is the widow of a prospector whose body was found in the Dragoons, and another is a wife whose husband gambled away all their money, then took off for parts unknown. She was stuck with no other way to live. There's no other work for them in this wonderful frontier town of yours. And I'm sure many, Josie included, are victims of child abuse who ran away from home. Josie won't talk about her past, but everything points to abuse."

"They can't all be poor, pathetic victims," he said, pushing a pillow behind his back. "Some of those gals are hardened criminals. Most of them have no concept of morals or decency."

This "old-fashioned" attitude again. Though Scott had no tolerance for "those gals," he did seem concerned about Josie's safety...because once she had been concerned about his.

"Josie writes poems, Scott, quite nice ones, really. I was privileged to read one."

Weighed down with concerns of his own, Scott seemed not to have heard. "Quite a few prostitutes must have prospectors for boyfriends," he mused.

Sarah moved her hand along his shoulder to his neck; there she could feel a strong pulse, the pulse of his heart beating faster because she was so close beside him. "You're thinking about your great-great-grandfather, aren't you? Wondering who his girlfriend is. It could be any of the younger girls, but it isn't so important, is it? I mean, it's not as if he married her."

"I have no way of knowing whether he married her or not. I don't know anything about my great-great-grandmother except that she was fair-haired."

"What was her name?"

He had to think for a minute. "Alma. There was so little about her."

Sarah smiled gently. "You sound worried about it. Isn't it rather redundant to worry about it now?"

"Well . . . a prostitute, though. What if he did marry her?"

"You're being judgmental. Do you see me flaunting my prejudice toward gunfighters?"

"That's different."

"Is it really so different?"

"Yeah. These women sell their bodies...."

"And I'm not so sure hired gunmen don't sell their souls."

Scott began to caress her body through the folds of the cumbersome white cotton nightgown. "We both have our own sets of values that can't change just because we changed centuries. I just keep wondering how long it will be before it all sinks in and feels like life instead of a game."

"It won't ever come to that. We won't stay long enough." She closed her eyes and luxuriated in the exploring hands.

"Damn it, Sarah," he said mildly. "I can't help how I feel. I've never been drawn to the seamy side of life. It's an embarrassment to me, your working there."

She opened her eyes. "Well, it's an embarrassment to me, your going around shooting people."

This plainly threw him. "I'm living like a man who can shoot and take care of himself."

"You love it."

"Sure I do. It's the experience of a lifetime. We agreed about . . ." He paused.

"Exactly," Sarah said. "We agreed, and now you're changing your mind."

"I think you're changing your mind, too."

Sarah scowled. "Maybe I am. Now that a growing number of hotheads want to try to get famous by outdrawing you."

He fell silent, unable to deny it.

"Maybe we should leave," she said.

"Leave?"

"Go home to our own century where we belong."

"Oh, come on. You're overreacting...." He was stroking her back now. "I like it here. I thought you did, too."

"The novelty is wearing off, and your attitude about my job is wearing thin."

"So is your attitude about *my* job," he said.

He's determined to stay in this hellhole, Sarah thought, panicking. The disagreement was liable to get serious. What if he was enjoying himself so much that he wouldn't listen to reason?

Scott's kiss interrupted that train of thought. Surrendering, Sarah doubted she could win a war with Scott MacInnes; he was too strong, and so was his effect on her. Until he came to his senses, she was trapped in a limbo of time already past, days already lived.

She couldn't get home without him.

Did he love her enough to take her back to their own time? Or was he determined to mold her into a woman who would fit properly into his life in 1882?

MORNING DAWNED brightly with rising excitement. Scott and Sarah were wakened by noise in the street—the sounds of horses, wagons and men's shouts. Sarah slid out of bed and pulled back the curtain.

"Word of the holdup must be all over town. A posse is forming on the corner."

Scott drew back the blanket and made a dash for his clothes. He was out the door in moments, strapping on his gun belt, giving her only a hurried peck on the lips for a goodbye.

Feeling a raw ache that came from a sense of not belonging, of being where they weren't supposed to be, she put on a robe Scott had bought for her, and made her way down the cold hallway to the bathroom.

In the Maison Dorée for breakfast an hour later, Sarah sat in her green velvet suit and flowered hat, drinking strong coffee and eating fried eggs. Everyone around her was talking about the loss of the payroll and cursing the lawlessness of Tombstone.

By eavesdropping, she learned that the dead man was indeed the dubious character from Dodge City they called Eagle Charlie. He had been shot and killed less than a mile from the site of the holdup. No one had seen his companion, Red Jake, who had ridden down with him from Dodge. Red Jake had obviously gotten greedy and decided not to share the loot. Now Jake was dodging a posse led by Federal Marshal Wyatt Earp and the rest of the Earp bunch. The bandit had had a head start of several hours, and no one knew where he was heading.

At the Bird Cage, Josie was in a strange mood. The shine was still in her eyes; unashamedly elated, she expressed relief when she learned of Charlie's death.

She remained elusive all day, and made herself scarce when the wave of miners came in. Sarah found her sitting backstage, the one place no customers could enter.

"I heard some guy was looking for you," Sarah said.

Josie had her book out again, trying to read in the poor light. Her hair hung around her shoulders and she was wearing a dress of black satin, the most somber gown Sarah had ever seen her in. "Too bad," Josie said. "I'm not available."

Sarah sat down beside her on a low bench. "Is anything wrong?"

"You saw the mood out there. Those rowdy men didn't get their pay. Not only are they broke, but they're feeling mean. I'll have none of them today."

"It was a cowboy who asked for you, not a miner."

"They can all go to hell," Josie said. "Like Charlie. I'll bet his feet are plenty hot right now. It's what he asked for. Even the devil wouldn't commend the likes of him."

"I see you have no respect for the dead," Sarah said lightly.

Josie smiled. "There's nothing respectable about being dead."

"Some friend his partner was. Did you know this Red Jake?"

"Not before they got to Tombstone." Josie closed her book. "It won't be easy trying to perform today. The audience will be difficult."

Sarah hadn't thought about that. "Then I won't do it. I can say to hell with them, too."

Josie grinned. "You got your cards handy? I'll challenge you to some gin rummy. We need whiskey to celebrate Charlie's demise. Would you get some, Sarah? If I go out there, I'll have to deal with customers."

"Sure. Why not? I'll let the jugglers and the sword-swallower take the brunt of the mood today."

She did only one short show that afternoon, to a restless, grumbling crowd. The mine manager had promised the pay would come, but it would take another week. She knew it was a rare miner who had a penny left from one payday to the next.

Before twilight, Scott came into the theater with some of the other posse members, and they gathered at the bar, talking about the day's search. The trackers had found no sign of Red Jake or the money. So the men of the posse, too, were in a foul mood.

Sarah knew Scott was here for the reason he came every night; he wanted to hear her sing. He wanted to keep an eye on her. She was sitting at a table under the balconies, telling fortunes, growing tired of dealing over and over again with the same questions about the holdup. Slipping her cards into the pocket of her gray skirt, she rose and made her way across the smoke-filled room to Scott.

Visibly surprised to see her not in costume, he circled an arm around her and offered her a drink, which she accepted, then stood beside him, listening to the discussion of the day's events.

Some moments later, trouble broke out in one of the balcony "cages." The curtains were drawn. Sarah had last seen Josie serving whiskey in the vicinity, walking across the catwalk with a man behind her. The man had had his hat well over his face and walked so close that the sleeve of his coat was touching her. Sarah had thought it curious, as Josie had said she wouldn't work today.

Onstage a lewd clown comedy act wasn't generating much laughter from the crowd, so the sounds of trouble in the box directly overhead were clearly heard.

"Josie's up there," Sarah said to Scott. "It sounds like a real fight."

He turned swiftly and hurried up the narrow steps at the side of the saloon to the catwalk that led to the cages. The noise grew louder, then a woman's scream came from behind the moving curtains. Moments later, the curtain trembled and Josie fell through. The clown act stopped. The audience looked up at the commotion.

Red Jake stood over Josie, holding a gun to her head. Before any of the posse members below could react, Scott burst into the cubicle. Jake turned his gun upon Scott. Not a sound could be heard from the smoke-filled room below; everyone waited for the gunshot. Sarah's knees buckled under her; she held on to a stranger for support.

"What good will it do you to shoot anybody?" Scott challenged Red Jake. "You'll never get out of here alive if you pull that trigger." He inched around, trying to create an opening for Josie to escape. "Why did you come back here when you had the money?"

"I ain't got the money!" Jake protested. "I ain't got nothin' and I didn't kill Charlie."

"You were seen by the stage driver." Scott kept his eye on the gun, not on the man, waiting for a chance to disarm him. The lawmen were probably making their way up the stairs by now. Red Jake didn't have a chance. He might kill Scott just to make a statement, but it was obvious Josie was the one he wanted dead.

Scott saw Jake push the gun closer to his chest, turn it toward Josie, then back to Scott, as if trying to decide which of them to shoot first.

"I wouldn't've shot Charlie," Jake growled at Josie in a voice so soft only she and Scott could hear. "Charlie was my onlyest pal." He waved the gun. "It was *her* done it! Her that got the money! Nobody else knew we was out there. The little bitch set us up and tried to kill us both, only I got away."

Scott glanced at Josie; she was paralyzed with fear. Red Jake wouldn't have come back if he'd had the money, Scott knew. He'd be over the Mexican border by now or headed north for Bowie. But what he was accusing Josie of seemed pretty unlikely.

Did it?

"It's her got the money," Red Jake repeated. "And her that's gonna tell me where it is."

"What good would it do you now? You won't get out of the Bird Cage, much less out of town." If Josie hadn't raised a fuss and the curtain fallen, Scott realized, Red Jake might have come and gone unidentified. He obviously intended to force Josie to reveal where the money was, then kill her.

Little Josie a killer and a robber? No. It was ridiculous.

Standing below, Sarah watched a couple of Earp's men sneak up the narrow catwalks, one on each side. Red Jake, visibly desperate by now, was flashing the gun in Josie's face, perspiration running from his brow. Terrified, Sarah knew Scott wouldn't stand hostage much longer; he would make a move.

Someone yelled from the floor, distracting the outlaw for a split second. Scott quickly drew his gun and shot the weapon from Jake's hand, a move he knew only a man with a short-barreled gun and three championship fast-draw trophies was capable of. Yowling in pain, the stage bandit doubled over, clutching his bleeding fingers and muttering a stream of curses. "She's the one . . . she's the one . . ." he gasped, but only Scott and Josie could hear him.

Josie turned and scurried over the catwalk, her black satin dress catching the light in soft flashes as she ran.

Lawmen converged on Red Jake and escorted the prisoner to Doc Goodfellow's office for medical attention. Scott was not among them. He knew the lawmen would assume it was only a matter of time until Red Jake confessed and they recovered the stolen cash.

Scott also knew this wouldn't happen.

Josie ran down the front steps and Sarah rushed to meet her at the bottom. "Are you all right, Josie?"

The girl looked at her wild-eyed. "He's crazy, that one," she said. "He would've shot me if your gunfighter hadn't come up. Why did he risk his life for the likes of me?" *It was Lucky's promise,* but Sarah could hardly say so. "That's the way he is," she answered instead.

"He's lucky he didn't get himself killed."

Sarah didn't want to think about that. The aftermath of fear began to catch up with Josie, and she shook violently, grasping Sarah's arm for support. "Scott is fast, Sarah," she said, breathing hard, as if not getting enough air, as if what she wanted to say to Sarah was very important. "No wonder they talk about him, and now they'll talk more than ever. I'm sorry for you. Someone will ambush him just to brag they were the one to get him. It's just a matter of time. I hate to tell you so, but you know it, anyway. I wish you and he would get out of this damned town."

Tears streamed down her cheeks as she spoke, tears Sarah didn't fully understand. Josie's moist eyes were sparkling as they'd sparkled last night; it was as if she had awakened to life again after a long, long time of being dead.

"Why was Jake after you?" Sarah asked.

"He's crazy, that's all I know. Only an idiot would have come back with the whole town looking for him." Josie took several deep breaths and wiped at her tears. "Sarah, listen. I'm going away. Please don't tell anybody I've left. It's not like anybody cares...you know...if I leave Tombstone, but don't tell, anyway.

They can wonder where I am tomorrow. You, though . . . you've been nice to me. I don't know why, but you were like a friend. So I want to say goodbye, but please don't look for me or tell anyone I've gone."

She seemed in a great hurry, but Sarah tried to delay her. "Are you going to meet your boyfriend?"

The girl nodded.

"Where is he?"

"I'm not sure, but I'll find him. Somewhere." She pulled away, forcing Sarah to loosen her grip. "I've wanted out of here, Sarah. I've wanted out so bad. . . ." She turned toward the front door of the crowded saloon, only glancing back quickly to say, "Don't tell . . . promise?"

"I promise. Josie, when will I—?"

She waved her hand. "Remember what I said. Get Scott out of this town before they carry him feet first up to Boot Hill."

Sarah watched Josie push her way through the crowd and felt a tug at her heart; it was the last time she would see her.

HALF AN HOUR LATER, Scott unlocked the door of their room. Sarah was sitting up in bed trying to keep warm, writing her journal in the light of the kerosene lamp.

"Why did you leave?" he asked.

"Why did you? I didn't expect you back for hours."

He locked the door and unfastened his gun belt. "I've got no reason to drink at the Bird Cage if you're not there."

Sarah looked at him sadly. "You saved Josie's life tonight. People will be talking about your quick draw for years. Maybe forever. You'll be one of Tombstone's legends."

"I can't be. I haven't been born yet."

"You might have been killed up there, Scott."

"He wasn't after me. He was after Josie. He thinks Josie shot Charlie and took the money."

"*What?*"

He sat on the edge of the bed and began the lengthy process of pulling off his boots. "Hell, maybe she did. I know Jake didn't have it."

"Josie? She couldn't." Even as she spoke, Sarah remembered Josie entering by the back door in the wee hours of the morning, all dressed in black. No, she told herself. She'd been with her boyfriend.

"Probably not," Scott agreed. He padded in his stocking feet across the room, lighted another lamp and examined the progress of his mustache.

"Determined to look like one of the Earp gang, are you?"

He wet his finger and smoothed the bristles. "Almost every man in town has a mustache, not just the Earp gang."

"They all look like weird clones with those huge handlebars. Very silly, if you ask me. Why are men so obsessed with growing masses of hair under their noses?"

He grew defensive. "Why do women wear hats that look like the aftermath of an explosion?"

Not smiling, she set down her tablet and pen. "Why do men become heroes because they foolishly risk their lives? What is the passionate lure of being a dead hero?"

Scott turned from the mirror, scowling. He took a small, string-tied bag of tobacco and a thin strip of paper from the dresser, licked the edge of the paper, and began patting tobacco from the pouch onto the paper.

"What the hell is *this* now?" Sarah wailed. "You don't smoke!"

He spilled tobacco over his hand and onto his lap. Disgusted, he dumped the whole mess. "You're in a great mood! Instead of being glad I got out of that theater confrontation alive, you just want to bitch at me. What's wrong with you?"

"You're right. We should celebrate your being alive. We'll celebrate every day that you're still alive. It's just a matter of time before . . . before . . ." She clenched her fists.

"Nobody's going to kill me," he said softly.

"Oh, really? That's no doubt what Morgan Earp is thinking, right now, down the hall in this very hotel. And it's almost March, Scott. Morgan has only three weeks to live! And last December, when they ambushed Virgil Earp outside the Oriental Saloon . . . it's only a miracle he didn't die. He's crippled for life from it, with a useless arm. Is that what you want to risk? What makes you think you're less vulnerable than the famous Earps?"

He had no response to this impassioned argument, he knew she was right. Murderers don't outdraw you in a duel; they get you from behind.

"Damn it, Sarah. It seems like all we do is argue, and always about the same thing. I know it was a close call tonight, but I didn't expect you to be so impossible once everything was all right. You left without even singing."

"Who could sing? It's been a terrible night. You and Josie nearly getting killed. And Josie's gone...."

Scott unbuttoned his jeans and pulled them off. "What do mean, Josie's gone?"

"Gone. She left. She wouldn't tell me where. To meet some guy, I think. But she's gone, and it's going to be awful without her around to talk to. I don't think I'll ever see her again."

"Gone?" he repeated. "That's damned interesting, in light of Red Jake accusing her of setting up him and Charlie."

Sarah straightened. "Everybody said Jake shot Charlie!"

"He didn't. Otherwise he wouldn't have been after Josie."

He sat down on the bed again, and she grabbed his arm. "Surely you don't believe Josie sneaked out there in the dark and shot Charlie!"

"I'm thinking about it. She knew the stage schedule. The man who was terrorizing her is dead from a bullet in the dark. Now you say she's left town. Why would she leave now, unless she had enough money to leave her job?"

"To meet her boyfriend."

"You don't know that for a fact, do you?"

"No, I only assumed it."

Scott smoothed his budding mustache again and spoke thoughtfully. "Maybe she figured they would kill her after the holdup, so there would be no witness against them. Maybe she figured it was her or them. She could have ridden out to the trees, waited until the bandits had the cash boxes and surprised them, intending to kill both, but only hitting Charlie. Maybe Jake rode off, scared for his life, and dropped the other cash box."

"That's . . . that's crazy!"

"What would a person do in her situation, Sarah? Wait for these bastards to kill her? Or double-cross them and get rid of them? I'm beginning to think that's exactly what she did."

Sarah blanched. "If you're right, she is carrying almost a hundred thousand dollars!"

"Money that belongs to the miners."

The chill of fear coursed through her. "Scott, you're not going to do anything about this! You're *not* going to try to recover that money! That girl has guts! She was completely cornered and she won! If you'd lived her life and risked everything, would you turn saint and give the money back to a mining company?" Sarah thumped her fist into her palm. "Way to go, Josie!"

"That's all well and good," Scott said mildly. "But the fact remains that she's stolen a hell of a lot of money. I wonder where she went?"

"It doesn't matter where she went. To her lover, I hope, if she has a lover. Yes, she does. She wrote that poem to him. It was pretty good, too. I read it five or six times because I felt it had hidden meanings." Sarah leaned back against the headboard and closed her eyes, trying to remember the lines. "'Yours is a distant land...strange tales you tell. I, too, come from far away, as far away as hell. You do not . . . you do not ask, you found my soul. Your eyes that love me know me well.'"

Silence descended over the room. Scott, sitting beside her, had fallen as mute as a corpse. The tobacco pouch he had picked up again fell from his hand.

Sarah opened her eyes to see him staring at her, then look away as if he had just seen a ghost. The expression on his face was so strange, she was afraid to ask what was wrong. Instead she waited.

At last he spoke. "Those lines . . . Josie's poem?"

Then she knew. "You've heard it before! Haven't you?"

"I've seen it." His voice was a monotone. "Among my grandfather's things." He brushed his hair from his forehead in the nervous gesture now familiar to Sarah.

"Then your great-great-grandfather did know Josie!"

"My God!" Scott exclaimed. "Josie!"

She swallowed. "Are you sure? You said her name was Alma."

He stared at the window. "My great-great-grandmother was named Alma Josephine. She wrote that poem to her husband."

11

SCOTT PUT HIS HEAD into his hands. They were shaking. "A prostitute."

Had it been a coincidence, Sarah wondered, that they'd befriended Josie in 1882 and not someone else? She suppressed an urge to put her arms around him and said instead, "Josie's a brave woman, Scott."

He didn't look at her.

"There must be a design," she continued. "Josie coming into your life, helping you when you needed help, and you helping her when she needed you. And don't forget it was Josie who gave me the bird she had treasured. If it weren't for her, we wouldn't be back here. There has to be some purpose. . . ."

"I don't get it," Scott said. "In the theater I thought I'd saved her life, but evidently I didn't. I mean, she lived, didn't she? She lived and took the holdup money and eventually married Ian MacInnes. And that money must have bought the ranch."

"It's hard to say what happened to it, Scott, or how they spent it. Ian made a rich strike, didn't he?"

Finally he looked up. "Yeah. It's all documented. I'd hate to think my family's landholdings were purchased with money stolen in a stage robbery. Although now I suppose some of it might have been."

"Maybe. Maybe not. There's no *proof* Josie had it."

Scott shook his head. "You don't have to try to protect me, Sarah. You're probably thinking I deserve this. Maybe it was somehow planned . . . by my great-great-grandmother."

She smiled. "So you might rethink your values. Josie was good to us and she didn't have to be. I only wish I could have talked to her more about her life, where she came from and how she ended up as a prostitute in Dodge City."

Scott sat in a heavy silence, visibly weighed down by his private thoughts.

"Surely it doesn't really bother you," Sarah said. "It can't matter now."

"I have no choice but to get used to the idea. The family covered this up. It would still cause a scandal if people knew."

"That's dumb—in our day and age."

He rolled his eyes. "Don't rub it in. It doesn't change the way I feel about you working at the Bird Cage Theater. My ancestor might have been employed there, but she, no doubt, had little choice."

"I'm on the verge of agreeing with you, now that the novelty is wearing off," Sarah admitted. "It was interesting with Josie there, but the atmosphere is getting to me. I've had about all the rowdiness I can take. Some slimy drunk cornered me this afternoon and wouldn't get his dirty hands off me."

Scott jerked to attention. "*What?* Who is he? Point him out to me, Sarah. I'll make sure he doesn't ever try anything again!"

"Oh, boy. The Lone Ranger rides!"

He gritted his teeth. "Don't pretend to shrug it off. I intend to find out who he is."

"I don't know who he is. Just a cowboy."

"A cowboy? Not a miner?"

"A rustler, probably. One of those tough types who always come in threes. Leave it, Scott. They were drinking and I was standing close to the edge of the stage."

His eyebrows raised. "He came up? Grabbed you onstage in front of everybody?"

Sarah pulled the blankets over her head, so he heard her reply muffled by the blankets. "I'm getting sick to death of this place! And now Josie is gone. When are we going back?"

"I don't want to go back yet," he declared angrily.

"And who made you the boss?"

"Damn it, Sarah, we just got here."

"We got here about three corpses ago! How many more are there going to be?"

"I don't know! It's not my fault this is a lawless town full of thieves and killers."

Sarah kept her head covered. It felt safer in the dark, where she couldn't see his determined eyes and the start of that mustache. How long did it take to grow those ugly things? He was planning to stay long enough for that . . . and how much longer? "It's a lawless town, all right. You don't have to get right in the middle—"

"Neither do you," he interrupted. "But you are, Sarah. You and your scandalous short pink skirt. Men at the ranch talk about your legs. Every man in town talks about your legs."

Sarah finally put her head out. Her hair was tousled and tangled and hung in her face. Under the blankets she'd been unable to see his angry eyes and for the first time had been able to hear the pain in his voice. She stared at him. He was honestly hurt by what she was doing. He didn't understand that it was the unique lure of the place . . . the wild excitement of the atmosphere. . . .

Oh, God . . . wasn't it the same wild excitement that attracted Scott to the circle of gunslingers? The lure of the romance of the past.

Maybe Scott's attitude was justified. A native Californian of the late twentieth century, she had grown up with bare legs and thought nothing of it. But this wasn't her world or her time. It was the Arizona Territory of the nineteenth century, and Scott understood the customs of the time far better than she did.

She'd considered this crazy jump back in time a wild, fantastic little adventure. It was more than that to Scott. His roots were here, his ancestors. He had some curious, unfinished business with the past.

The past had a lot to tell Scott about himself. He seemed to sense that, always had.

Now he'd learned more than he wanted to know.

"I've been a little stupid about taking chances," she said softly. "Especially with the costume."

The look in his eyes was one of confusion mingled with hurt, and there was no spark of victory at her admission. "Why not quit and let me take care of you?"

"Your wages aren't as high as mine."

"I have a lot more than wages. Bringing in outlaws for the rewards pays very well. There are plenty more rewards to be claimed. And I've got information nobody else has."

She gave him a shove. "Nothing you could do would be more dangerous!"

"It's a living."

"Damn it," Sarah said; it was useless.

"Why not just do the fortune-telling at a side table?" he suggested. "You seem to have become an expert at combining historical events with your own fantasies."

"I can't make much doing that."

"Oh, I don't know. There'll be a mine accident in a couple weeks, a cave-in near a part called Crazy Stem or Crazy Bend, something like that. You can warn the company and hopefully prevent it."

"If it's prevented, there won't be an accident to foretell, will there? All these things we know about...these dangers..."

Her voice faded. Sarah hugged her knees. For her, the novelty of 1882 had worn off and nothing felt right anymore. It was horrible to know the future.

"What about Morgan Earp?" she asked Scott after a long silence. "Do I tell him not to go to Robert Hatch's

after the theater on March 18? He might pay no attention if I did. Or else he might not go and then get shot
wherever he _does_ go, and I could conceivably get
blamed for his death. Remember Doc Holliday's ram-
page after Morgan's death? I shudder to even think of
getting in the middle of that. What do we do, Scott?"

"I don't know...." Despair rasped his voice. "If we
start altering history, we won't be able to predict it
anymore."

SCOTT RODE OUT, looking for some outlaws who had
robbed a gun store in Benson. He knew who they were;
he also knew they wouldn't be captured for another
week, so he had a chance to bring them in early. From
the sidewalk in front of the Cosmopolitan, Sarah
watched him ride down Allen Street in the middle of the
morning, and stop in front of the OK Corral to talk to
Deputy Marshal Wyatt Earp.

She saw women turn to look at the tall, handsome
cowboy. Members of rustler gangs squinted and glared
at the man whose short-barreled, strange-looking gun
was becoming a legend—a gun every one of them cov-
eted, Sarah knew.

Her fear for his safety grew each day. Here he was,
going searching for outlaws. Searching for trouble.
Would he come back tonight? Tomorrow?

If Scott got himself killed, would she then be stuck
here forever? _I want out of here!_ a voice within her
screamed. Scott, curse him, was determined to stay.

THAT NIGHT she abandoned her short costume, in spite of Hutchinson's wishes, and performed in one of the three dresses Josie had left—the maroon satin she had worn when eleven-year-old Sally first saw her. Leaving the dance-hall costumes meant Josie was leaving her dance-hall life behind. It was further proof she had something better to go to.

Two customers had asked after her, but she had been gone less than twenty-four hours, which wasn't long enough to arouse any suspicion that she'd left Tombstone for good. Maybe there would be no concern at all over her sudden disappearance; maybe Josie was right and no one cared. The owner would simply find a replacement among the hundreds of girls who wanted to work at the Bird Cage.

Halfway through her second song, Sarah caught sight of the man who had harassed her onstage the night before. He wasn't acting drunk this time, so she wasn't prepared for what happened next.

The cowboy, egged on by his companions, bounded up the stairs at the front of the stage, turned to the audience for applause, grabbed Sarah and fondled her breasts. She shrieked and tried to pull away, but his grip was too strong. A few men cheered. Others shouted at him to get away from her.

Struggling to free herself, she could smell the sweaty odor of his unwashed body. Her stomach churned.

Scott leaped onto the stage. He grabbed the grinning cowboy, pulled him away, and punched him. Immediately the stage was overrun by the rustler's friends, and fists were flying. In seconds a full-fledged riot was under way. Sarah backed away, horrified. One of the rustler gang drew a knife, but Scott didn't see it and was stabbed in the hand.

Gunshots broke up the fight. Billy Hutchinson, flanked by lawmen, threatened to shoot the next man who moved. Scott, wiping blood from his mouth with his bleeding hand, glared at the man who had gone after Sarah.

"I intend to kill you," he said into the new, shaky silence.

To save face, the outlaw had no choice but to accept the challenge.

Sarah, coming up behind Scott in time to hear the threats and see the blood, panicked. The last time this had happened—when an eleven-year-old was stabbed, trying to protect her—he had been carried from the site. This time whoever was carried away would be dead!

"Don't do this!" she pleaded. "You're wounded!'

"No man attacks my woman and gets away with it." The anger in his eyes was so fierce, it silenced her. Momentarily Sarah knew the code of honor of the West wouldn't let Scott back down.

"You've lost your mind!" she yelled at the cowboy she loved.

But she could feel the excitement rising. A crowd formed around the gunfighters to escort them into the street. One of the Bird Cage women offered Scott a clean handkerchief, which he tied around his bleeding hand with the help of one of the wranglers from the

Double Bar Z. Sarah watched in disbelief, shaking so hard she couldn't have helped with the makeshift bandage, had she tried.

The crowd almost carried the challengers toward the front entrance. Scott turned to meet Sarah's eyes. His hand reached out and she reached back. Words formed on her lips. "Please don't. . . ."

"I'll be okay," he assured her, pressing her hand with his good one. In the noise she couldn't hear his voice, but knew the words; they seemed quite meaningless. Scott had no way of knowing.

She had no time to try to separate fear from disbelief. Sarah stood outside the Bird Cage along with the rest of the crowd, and watched the man she loved walk into the middle of the street, the handle of the gun in his holster glinting in the light of a street lamp.

The two men faced off. Seconds later two shots rang out, one far ahead of the other, and the man called Stretch lay on the ground, not moving.

People were running toward the fallen cowboy. Scott must have assumed his adversary was dead, because he made no attempt to find out. With his automatic he could have fired half a dozen bullets in the time a revolver could fire two, but he hadn't. He had shot only once, right through the other man's chest. He returned the pistol to its holster and turned away.

His eyes met Sarah's. She saw no look of victory, only the remnants of seething anger.

What he saw in her eyes was a desolate sadness. A man was dead.

The crowd didn't seem overly concerned, except for two companions of Scott's latest victim. Sarah saw them look at Scott with a hatred unlike any she had ever encountered.

Oh, God, she thought, *this thing isn't over!*

Scott walked straight toward her. His face was grim. Busy checking the blood-soaked handkerchief on his hand, he was paying no heed to the onlookers swarming around him. Even with the wounded hand, the draw had not been close.

"Let's get out of here," he said to Sarah.

Without a word she fell into step beside him. Her legs were trembling so, she had to grab Scott's arm for support. They passed the Lion Brewery and several saloons, crossed Fifth street and entered the Crystal Palace. A few men were sauntering back inside, and the pianist was resuming the music. Scott led her to a table in the center and pulled out a chair.

A waiter came rushing toward them. Did he know that his customer was the victor in the duel? "Two whiskeys," Scott said.

"Yes, sir! On the house!"

Sarah felt as if everyone in the place was gawking at them—at the gunfighter who'd just sent another cowboy to meet his maker, and at the woman in dance-hall clothes sitting with him.

She was too shocked to speak. Scott, too, was quiet.

At last she asked, "How bad is your hand?"

"I don't think it's bad." He pulled the kerchief from his neck and began wrapping it around the bloody handkerchief.

"What are you doing? Let me see it."

"I'll have it looked at later, not here. As long as I can move all my fingers, I know the cut can't be all that serious."

"Does it hurt badly?"

"It's starting to. We'll just have a couple whiskeys and then leave. I need a drink."

"That was crazy, shooting with a wounded hand," she said softly while she helped him tie a knot in the kerchief.

"The guy was slow as a sloth."

"The next one might not be."

The waiter brought the whiskeys in a hurry. Visibly excited he set them down spilling whiskey over a tattoo on his wrist. Sarah gazed at the image of a coiled serpent and shuddered.

He pulled a bar towel from his belt and patted the table. "Sorry for spilling your drink, ma'am. I'll bring another."

"Bring two more while you're at it," Scott said, and drank his in one long gulp.

"How can you be so calm after killing a man?"

"What a man feels inside doesn't show."

That seemed to be true. Sarah tried to read his eyes and couldn't. "But you have no regrets."

"He shouldn't have touched you...and he shouldn't have challenged me."

"Scott..."

His eyes examined her and she fell silent. "You look like a prostitute in that dress."

"I'm sure I do. It's Josie's dress. It covers my legs, damn it. What do you want from me?"

"I've told you a dozen times. I want you out of the Bird Cage. What happened tonight just proves my point. You were standing up there like an apple waiting to be picked. Aren't you convinced yet that it's dangerous? And now...here...in that satin dress...people will think of you as the kind of entertainer you don't want to be."

Disgusted, she answered, "A gunfighter's whore, that's what I must look like. They probably think we're a good match."

He glared at her. "You're not going back there again where you can be mauled by the likes of—" He paused. "What do you call a man who's just died?"

What would have happened, Sarah wondered, *if Scott had not been there?* Would anyone else have risked the wrath of the cowboy gang to save her?

"Where do we go from here, Scott? Is my singing career over, then? You could protect me, but I suppose you'll kill every man who looks at me sideways."

"I suppose I will."

Tears began to sting behind her eyes, but she fought them back and refused to allow herself to cry. "How can I love a killer?" she whispered.

He blinked as if she had slapped him.

"I don't know what's happened to you," she said. "This damned fast-gun obsession everybody has here is just . . ." She paused, still struggling with the tears. "Scott, you've ruined my life. My whole life. I fell in love with you when I was eleven and I've loved you ever since. I could never find another guy who could live up to what you were . . . what you were to me. I searched for someone like you all my life and finally found you. And for a little while I was so ecstatically happy I didn't care what else was going on or where we were. But then you got . . . got caught up in this life that isn't even real to me and made yourself the target of every outlaw and would-be gunslinger in the Territory. Now I get to wait for you to be the next one killed. Every day I get to wonder if that day is your last. How dare you do this to me! How dare you ruin my life, when all I've ever done is love you!"

Scott stared across the table as if in shock.

"All right," she conceded. "So I did one thing to you. I sang at a bordello and you weren't pleased about that. I didn't take up quilting and jam-making and wear a calico bonnet! But how could I have done those things? How could you expect me to be a—a frontier woman?"

After a long, painful silence, Scott said, "I didn't mean to ruin your life."

"Well, you have. And if I choose to sing instead of knit shawls for the short time I have left before I go insane, then that's just too darn bad."

Scott felt a sharp pain. He had been worried about what would happen to *her* in the theater, but how much

cause was he giving her to worry even more? He had
been so caught up in the romance of Old Tombstone
and being part of it that he had been convinced Sarah
was just as enthralled. If he'd really listened to her, he
would have known better.

He'd wanted to protect her, give to her, make her
happy. Instead, he'd followed the dreams of his youth
as blindly as he had as a boy. He'd recreated the days of
lawlessness, made heroes of men whose only claim to
greatness had been the fact that they could shoot faster
than other men. As Tombstone's latest "living legend,"
he'd never had so much fun in his life, but knew deep
inside he was playing a child's game—a deadly child's
game. He had eased into this life so naturally, thriven
on it, and relished the rush of excitement in his blood,
more convinced than ever that he'd always belonged
here. But Sarah . . .

He reached for her hand. "Sarah, will you marry
me?"

"What?"

"Marry me. And let me be a husband to you, the way
it should be."

Yes! screamed her heart. Her heart screamed out her
love, the love of a lifetime. Knowing he wanted to be
with her forever, she wanted him more than she wanted
life.

But she was scared. "Are you asking as the one last
desperate attempt to get me out of the Bird Cage?"

"Yes. And no. I'm asking because I want to marry
you. There has never been another woman for me and

there never will be. We both know that. I want you to be my wife."

"I'll be a widow."

He clutched her hand tighter. "We belong together."

Sarah could no longer hold back the tears. She grasped his hand as if hanging on to life. "I want to marry you. I will marry you, Scott, of course I will! But not here. Not in 1882. Let's go back, please. Let's go home."

"You won't marry me here?"

"No, I won't."

"Never?"

"What do you mean, never? Surely you don't plan to stay here forever?"

"I haven't thought about leaving so soon. . . ."

Feeling eyes on them, Scott glanced about the room. An old cowboy with a wide, flat hat and gray curls around his ears was standing at the far end of the bar, leaning on his elbows and looking at them. His weathered face was vaguely familiar, but he couldn't place the man.

Sarah shifted to see what he was looking at. Just another cowboy, probably in his seventies, alone with a hand-rolled cigarette and a whiskey glass.

"Who is he?" she asked.

"I don't know. . . ." Scott turned his attention back to her. "I haven't thought of leaving," he repeated. "I didn't realize how unhappy you were. I thought you were still excited about being here. You won't marry me in Tombstone?"

She wanted to marry him now, this moment, but answered, "In Tombstone, yes. In 1882, no."

"You mean I have to choose between this...and you?"

Between death and a long life with me, she wanted to say, but the words stuck in her throat. Did she have the right to make him such an ultimatum?

"I'd rather have you," he said. "If you aren't happy living here, then I can't be, either. Your happiness is more important to me."

She grasped his hand, dizzy with relief. "Scott, are you sure?"

He smiled. "I can't ask you to knit shawls. And I can't risk getting shot and leaving you here alone." He finished the whiskey that stood untouched in her glass. "What if we can't get back?"

"Don't say that!"

"It's something I've worried about. How do we know it'll work again?"

"It has to work!" Sarah felt the color drain from her face. "Let's go back now, today. I saw how some of those cowboys looked at you after the gunfight. They wanted to kill you on the spot. I can't take any more of it. I just want out of here."

"First I want to talk to Morgan—" he began. One of the wranglers of the Double Bar Z rushed to the table, out of breath.

"MacInnes! Johnny Ringo is looking for you. He says he intends to kill you!"

"Ringo? What are you talking about?"

"That Stretch Cates you just killed was Ringo's pal. Some folk say he was his best friend."

"Ringo never had a best friend." Scott scowled, fully aware of the danger this frantic message contained. Johnny Ringo was a hothead, a ruthless outlaw who liked trouble as much as he liked whiskey. Unfortunately for a lot of people, he was fast with his gun.

"Ringo's saying you gunned down Stretch without giving him a chance. He swears he can take you down."

"He's too big a coward to face me in a fair duel."

The wrangler's voice rose with excitement. "He's had a couple drinks. Everybody knows how dangerous Ringo is when he's mad. Hell, he even challenged Doc Holliday!"

"He was drunk and the duel never happened."

"That's because Wyatt interfered. This time Ringo thinks he has a good reason to kill you . . . for murdering his pal. He's looking for you." He turned and left them.

Sarah leaned across the table. "Everyone knows Johnny Ringo is a crazy killer! We have to leave before this goes any further!"

"I don't think Ringo can outdraw me."

"Really? Look how your gun hand is bleeding!" She rose abruptly. "And who cares which of you can draw a gun faster? Are you coming with me or not?"

They walked out of the Crystal Palace and down Allen Street toward the Bird Cage Theater. "The birds are hidden at the back of the stage," she said. "Let's get them and leave."

"I'd feel like I was running from a fight. A man doesn't run from a fight."

"Fight Ringo with a wounded hand? Have you lost your mind?"

"It's a matter of honor."

"Honor? Among thugs like Ringo? I can't marry honor! Be fair to me, Scott! We agreed to leave."

There were more people than usual on the street, not a good sign. Word was probably out about Ringo's challenge. They entered the Bird Cage and pushed through the crowd. Sarah led the way to the stage.

She hurried up the stairs, thankful that Scott hadn't stopped to talk to any of his cowboy friends. Some dancing girls were ready to appear onstage. No one was in the far reaches of the backstage area, behind the inner curtain and props, where Sarah had hidden the china birds.

The birds were still safe. She retrieved the handbag and was lifting out the first little bird when a figure appeared without warning at the top of the back stairs. He stood legs apart, elbows resting on two leather holsters that hung from his loose-fitting trousers. A tall, good-looking man with blue eyes, a wide mustache and sandy-red hair.

Johnny Ringo.

Sarah was so startled, she didn't realize the glass bird had slipped from her hands until she heard the tiny sound of breaking glass.

The bird lay in two pieces at her feet.

12

SARAH STARED at the two pieces—their chance to get back to the world they belonged in destroyed.

Horrified, she glanced at Scott. He, too, had been looking at the broken bird instead of the dark-clad outlaw. Their eyes met for a moment of dismal comprehension. Then Johnny Ringo stood in front of them, clearly determined that Scott should die.

Sarah's life flashed before her. Would her family, her friends never know what had happened to her?

Were she and Scott stuck in a boomtown that would live only a few more years before the mines closed and the town began to decay? Would Scott even live until tomorrow's sunrise?

Ringo's voice broke the strange silence. "You heard I was looking for you, MacInnes? You trying to hide out behind the stage curtains?"

Sarah realized at once why Ringo was falsely thought to be an educated man. His speech was careful and articulate.

Scott's full, deep voice came like a boom of thunder. "You're braver drunk than sober, Ringo. My advice is not to start trouble with me."

The outlaw grinned. "I'm a man who likes trouble. But I don't like it when a friend of mine gets gunned down in cold blood."

"Half the town witnessed a fair duel," Scott replied evenly. "As for you—a man should know his limitations."

The tall, slender Ringo laughed and looked his adversary up and down. "So Stretch's bullet hit your hand, did it?"

"This is no bullet wound. His bullet hit the dust while he was falling."

Sarah listened to the exchange in disbelief. It was like being inside a film, with all the sights and sounds. Not real, yet horribly real. And leading to a fight. Sarah knew how Johnny Ringo had died—and it hadn't been by a gunman named MacInnes. She had to get Scott out of here!

Desperate now, she bent to gather the broken pieces of the bird. It was the one she'd given Scott, the one he called a sparrow. *Only pieces, but maybe the magic would still work.* With the whole bird in one hand and the pieces in the other, she inched toward Scott under the watchful eyes of the killer.

Whatever else he was—whatever fables had been told about him—Ringo was a man who throve on killing. His blue eyes shone with evil. Sarah trembled with fear as she drew her arm around Scott's and clasped the birds wing to wing. *Now,* she prayed. *Now!*

Nothing happened.

The bird was broken and the magic gone.

Her body grew cold. *Let this be a horrible dream*, she begged the powers that had brought them here. *This can't be happening . . . it can't!*

"This is plain touching," Ringo said. "Your woman trying to protect you."

Scott pulled the kerchief off his right hand. Underneath, the once-white handkerchief was red. He flexed the hand, glaring at his opponent. "Who's talking about needing protection?"

Numb, Sarah backed away from Scott and faced the outlaw. It was clear now what Scott meant and why Ringo had stood there so long; he had been waiting for backup. His backup had just arrived; two men stood on the stairs. Members of his rustling gang, no doubt, and they would have their guns aimed at Scott's head. This would not be a fair fight.

"You probably heard I can see the future," she said, struggling to keep her voice from shaking. "And I can see your death, Mr. Ringo."

"Good try." He was plainly enjoying this. "But I don't believe in witches."

Scott had to be angry. Sarah knew he couldn't back away from Ringo's challenge and still go on living in Tombstone. And he *would* have to go on living here; the magic that had transported them through time was gone.

Sarah was terrified. She hadn't lied about knowing of Ringo's death. He would be found dead in Turkey Creek Canyon with a bullet hole through his head . . . but not until next July. That meant he would still be alive at the end of this bleak February day. And if he was alive at the end of this night, Scott would not be.

She stepped closer to Scott again. "You can't go through with a duel!"

He didn't answer.

"Turkey Creek Canyon!" she reminded him. "July. *July,* Scott!"

He ignored her warning. "You can't outdraw me," he said to Ringo. "You're welcome to try only if you're ready to die."

"Scott!" Panic edged Sarah's voice. She could hear it as she spoke. Scott would be facing three men. He could not get out of this alive. He must know that. He was trying to scare Ringo, to bluff his way out. *Wasn't he?* Or did he really believe he could win this fight when he knew Ringo had another five months to live?

Did he think he could change history? *Could* he?

She didn't think so. He was going to die. If not from Ringo's bullet, then from one from his gang. Desperate, still clasping the magical birds, she felt the strap of her handbag on her arm. It reminded her that she had always carried a small knife. Feeling around inside the purse, she couldn't find the knife, but did find an open package of chewing gum. Four sticks were left.

Chewing gum.

Muttering a prayer while her trembling hands unwrapped a stick of gum, she was conscious of Ringo watching her curiously, saying nothing. He seemed to be waiting for Scott to make a move toward the stage steps, to lead the way into the street.

John Ringo smiled and spoke. "Lead the way, MacInnes."

"I don't want you at my back, Ringo. I'm told you aren't above shooting a man in the back."

Sarah stuffed the gum into her mouth and chewed frantically, her mouth dry. Shakily holding the sparrow, she pulled out the gum and stuck it onto the neck of the headless bird.

"Nobody accuses me of cowardice and lives!" Ringo moved toward the stairs, hands inches from his pistols, ready to draw at the slightest additional provocation.

Scott stood rigid and alert, his hand near his holster, his eyes fixed on the angry killer. "You can back out of this, Ringo, and no one will be the wiser for it. I've killed one man today. I don't fancy killing another, but I will if I have to."

Carefully—as carefully as her trembling hands would let her—Sarah fitted the head onto the glob of gum, turning it to the proper angle and smoothing her thumb and forefinger over the gum-filled crack to make sure the fit was exactly right. "Scott, come back with me! Try!" she pleaded.

"I have to see this through," he muttered. "I can do it."

You can't! she wanted to scream. She dropped the handbag onto the floor and moved in next to Scott, holding the mended bird in one hand and the whole one in the other. "Take it! Please!"

He didn't.

"Today is February 27! Ringo is not going to die to-day!" she whispered.

Scott turned slowly from the gloating outlaw and looked at her. In his eyes she saw confusion—and love.

She shoved the crudely mended sparrow at him. "Take it! It's our only chance to be together!"

She pressed it into his hand and felt his fingers fold over it. Sarah held the other figurine against his; their wings touched, just as they had on that long-ago day, here, on this very spot, when she'd given the little magic treasure to Lucky.

A sudden blackness. As it descended, she felt him grasp her free hand and hold on. It was as if a black curtain had fallen from the top flies of the stage and covered everything with a layer of darkness so heavy they could feel its weight. With it fell a deep silence.

Sarah felt dizzy. It was the familiar dizziness, born of a sensation of spinning rapidly and far. Scott was still holding her hand.

THE SILENT DARKNESS slowly lifted. Out of the shadows rose the smell, the sounds of age. Dust, mildew and unidentifiable echoes. Scott was beside her.

He was holding her hand. Both little glass sparrows, one with its head slightly askew, were still with them. The curtains were gone, and the theater was as deathly silent as the gold-trimmed hearse that stood at the back of the stage behind them. The hearse that had once carried the dead to their final resting place on Boot Hill.

Dazed, Scott studied the broken bird, its head stuck on with chewing gum, and then Sarah, whose hand was gripping his so tightly he could feel her fingernails digging into his skin.

"Out of the corner of my eye I saw both guys behind Ringo reach for their guns," he said softly. "I think I owe my life to you, Sarah."

She still felt dizzy and out of breath. "I was afraid you thought you could take all three."

"I'm not quite that crazy."

Both were disoriented; it was like standing on solid ground after months at sea. The time that had been was still too much with them . . . still alive.

"This theater," she said, shuddering. "Those echoes! Do you hear them, Scott? The echoes?"

"The ghosts," he said.

She looked around. A tall shadow moved in one of the cages. Near the railing of the stairway, where Johnny Ringo had been standing, the air was ice-cold. And below, near the piano, came a glint of gold, like light on metal, reflected off something unseen.

"The ghosts..." she repeated. "This place is still alive and yet so horribly dead!"

"I think we need to get out of here."

A party of tourists entered through the small door at the far end of the room. Sarah, realizing she was still wearing Josie's old-fashioned dress, panicked. But the tourists only smiled, said enthusiastic hellos and moved their attention to the cages above their heads, where a few manikins had been placed in nineteenth-century costumes.

She glanced at the gun on Scott's hip and gave him an inquiring look.

He smiled. "It's probably Sunday. Helldorado Days. There are people walking all over Tombstone in costumes. They put on skits for the tourists."

She winced. "Gunfights, I suppose."

"Absolutely."

"You wouldn't . . . not today."

He laughed. "No. I've had enough gunfighting for one lifetime."

She hugged him. "We made it back! Oh, thank God! We made it back! I was scared to death."

Incredulous, he shook his head and held her tight. "Johnny Ringo. Who the hell would have thought it . . . ?"

"We were saved by a wad of chewing gum. What a story, and we can't even tell anyone. No one would ever believe us."

"It doesn't matter. You and I believe it." He took her hand. "Let's get out of here."

He led her through the theater and out the narrow doorway into what only moments ago had been a noisy, boisterous saloon. The carved wooden bar was still there, along with the bullet-damaged, nine-foot-tall painting of Fatima, a well-endowed, scantily clad dance-hall girl. The railed catwalk above that led to the cages was still there. Only the people were gone.

The tourists milling about smiled at their clothes and the bloody handkerchief on Scott's hand, clearly believing they were costumes for the local celebration. Still trying to get used to the effect of crossing the time barrier, Sarah said, "It seems more traumatic to make a jump forward than a jump back. Do you feel it, too?"

"Yeah. Imagine somebody jumping forward if they *started* in the past. Now that would be even harder to take!"

It was a crisp February evening. Down at the far end of Allen Street, in front of the OK Corral, a gunfight was being staged and people were gathered on either side. Music came from the Crystal Palace Saloon.

"I've forgotten where we parked," she said.

"We've been gone so long I'll have a parking ticket and everybody will be frantic looking for me. I'm in no mood to face all that."

"We don't know for sure how long we've been gone. We don't know what day it is."

"That's so." He stopped at the corner, at the open doors of the saloon. "Let's go in here."

"The Crystal Palace? This seems so odd, Scott! We were just in here! Right over there at that table."

"That was a hundred years ago," he said, heading for the same table. He held a chair for her and ordered two beers.

A singer was strumming a guitar on a small platform, and the bar was filled with tourists wearing bright-colored sweatshirts. It was the same enormous

Palace bar in front of the same enormous mirrors, but the sounds were not the same, the feel was different.

Had Scott changed in the switch of time, Sarah wondered, as he had when they went the other way? Was he the same man she had come to know? The gunfighter?

His blue eyes examined her. "A century ago we sat at this very spot. I asked you to be my wife and you said yes. But circumstances were completely different then."

Already she could feel the pain; her heart was starting to break. He must have changed his mind. "Completely different," she admitted.

"Would you still say yes, in 1992?"

"Would you ask in 1992?"

"That's why I wanted to come back into the Crystal Palace. To ask you again in our century. To update the offer." He reached for her hand. "Could you be happy living on a horse ranch in southern Arizona?"

Life has just become real, she thought. Sarah pictured pink sky behind the Arizona mountains and the view from his bedroom. She pictured them walking together under the cottonwood trees....

"We belong together," she answered. "I belong wherever you are. I said yes a hundred years ago, and through all those years I haven't stopped loving you."

His eyes brightened with more joy than she had ever seen in them. "What about your career?"

"I can write in Tombstone."

There was nothing more to consider, nothing more to know. She and Lucky were together for always. It was a moment she had dreamed of a thousand times. Had the magical birds promised less?

The waiter brought their beers and set down the icy mugs in front of them. On his right hand a tattooed snake coiled its way over his wrist. Sarah started. The same tattoo! She looked up.

It was the same waiter.

Her heart began to pound. Scott looked as though he was seeing a ghost. "Wait . . ." he demanded.

The waiter grinned; it was clear he knew them. He gave them a strange salute and went back to his work, taking an order from another table.

Baffled, Sarah and Scott sat in silence, looking at him over the heads of the tourists.

Scott touched her arm and nodded toward the end of the bar. The old, grizzled cowboy with the flat hat and rolled cigarette was leaning on the bar in the same spot he had been before, a hundred years earlier. The same face, the same clothes. The same man.

The old-timer looked up and his eyes met theirs. He smiled a knowing smile. Above his head was a sign that read: Tombstone, Arizona—the Town Too Tough to Die.

So they were not the only ones who'd crossed over into Tombstone's scandalous and dangerous past! Others had done it, too . . . and now walked among the unsuspecting tourists, who felt the presence of ghosts without knowing why. Just as Sarah had felt their presence during her first moments in the Bird Cage Theater.

Scott squeezed the hand of his bride to be. "We aren't alone!" he said.

"What does it all mean?" she whispered over the pounding of her heart.

"I don't know. I only know it's a haunted town. I only know strange forces made it our destiny to find each other. Maybe we were supposed to meet a century ago and our destinies caught on the winds of the years, kind of like seeds that had to find the right place to grow and flower.

Her eyes misted. "You sound like a poet."

"Maybe I inherited the gift from my great-great-grandmother."

"I think," she mused, "Josie wanted you to know her."

"But I was too stubborn. I only knew her through you.... I think Josie loved you." He caressed her with his eyes. "I love you, Sarah. I've loved you for a long, long time. Even longer than you know."

HARLEQUIN®

Temptation®

Rebels & Rogues

Jared: He'd had the courage to fight in Vietnam. But did he have the courage to fight for the woman he loved?

THE SOLDIER OF FORTUNE
By Kelly Street
Temptation #421, December

All men are not created equal. Some are rough around the edges. Tough-minded but tenderhearted. Incredibly sexy. The tempting fulfillment of every woman's fantasy.

When it's time to fight for what they believe in, to win that special woman, our Rebels and Rogues are heroes at heart. Twelve Rebels and Rogues, one each month in 1992, only from Harlequin Temptation.

HARLEQUIN®

Temptation®

the Fortune Boys

A funny, sexy miniseries from bestselling
author Elise Title!

**LOSING THEIR HEARTS MEANT
LOSING THEIR FORTUNES....**

If any of the four Fortune brothers were unfortunate enough to
wed, they'd be permanently divorced from the Fortune
millions—thanks to their father's last will and testament.

BUT CUPID HAD OTHER PLANS!
Meet Adam in #412 **ADAM & EVE** (Sept. 1992)
Meet Peter #416 **FOR THE LOVE OF PETE**
(Oct. 1992)
Meet Truman in #420 **TRUE LOVE** (Nov. 1992)
Meet Taylor in #424 **TAYLOR MADE** (Dec. 1992)

**WATCH THESE FOUR MEN TRY TO WIN
AT LOVE AND NOT FORFEIT $$$**

HARLEQUIN HISTORICAL
CHRISTMAS
·STORIES·1992·

Capture the magic and romance of Christmas in the 1800s
with HARLEQUIN HISTORICAL CHRISTMAS STORIES
1992, a collection of three stories by celebrated historical
authors. The perfect Christmas gift!

Don't miss these heartwarming stories, available in
November wherever Harlequin books are sold:

MISS MONTRACHET REQUESTS by Maura Seger
CHRISTMAS BOUNTY by Erin Yorke
A PROMISE KEPT by Bronwyn Williams

Plus, as an added bonus, you can receive a FREE keepsake
Christmas ornament. Just collect four proofs of purchase
from any November or December 1992 Harlequin or
Silhouette series novels, or from any Harlequin or
Silhouette Christmas collection, and receive a beautiful
dated brass Christmas candle ornament.

Mail this certificate along with four (4) proof-of-purchase coupons plus $1.50 postage and
handling (check or money order—do not send cash), payable to Harlequin Books, to: **In the
U.S.:** P.O. Box 9057, Buffalo, NY 14269-9057; **In Canada:** P.O. Box 622, Fort Erie, Ontario,
L2A 5X3.

**ONE PROOF OF
PURCHASE**

Name: _____

_____

Address: _____

_____

City: _____

State/Province: _____

Zip/Postal Code: _____

HX92POP   093 KAG